Treachery At Stylex

By:

Morton Erstling

www.syppublishing.com

Southern Yellow Pine
Publishing

Published by
Southern Yellow Pine (SYP) Publishing
4351 Natural Bridge Rd.
Tallahassee, FL 32305

www.syppublishing.com

Copyright: Morton Erstling Estate 2013
Cover photo Copyright: Oliver Sved/Shutterstock.com
Cover Design: Taylor Nelson

ISBN-10: 0985706260

ISBN-13: 978-0-9857062-6-5

Printed in the United States of America
First Edition - August 2013

Dedication

Morton Erstling
May 30, 1931 - May 31, 2013

To my wonderful husband, author of this book, known for his intellect, gentle spirit, kindness, generosity, and extraordinary sense of humor. A man adored by his family and friends.

With love always,

Sheila

Morton Erstling passed away during the editing process of this novella. It is being published posthumously. One of his lifelong dreams was to write and publish a fiction book. His wife, Sheila Erstling, chose to continue the project to completion. She wanted his dream to become a reality. She also wanted his family of four children and eight grandchildren to have this memory for the future. The following poem is by his granddaughter.

Grandpa

People say it's hard to write a poem,
Just a difficult thing to do,
But it will be nothing of the sort,
With someone as amazing as you.

Your newspaper crosswords,
And your marble game,
Don't forget Sudoku books,
More puzzles than you can name.

Your very patient temperament,
And encouraging mood,
When doing mind boggling games,
Something you're willing to teach and do.

You draw like a master,
You didn't even need to take a class,
If I were your teacher,
In one second you would pass.

The pink wooden flamingo,
And my name made out of shells,
The amazing pictures of me,
Good enough to sell.

You fall asleep during anything,
And just for you to hear,
I have to say things three more times,
Right into your ear.

I love when you come to visit,
Even if we just snuggle on a chair
With your caring heart and brilliant mind
We make quite a pair.

I love you, Emma

Introduction

Stylex Custom Hardware Company manufactures hardware for kitchens, bathrooms, and closets. Some of these items include; cabinets, faucets, toilets, bidets, shower stalls, bathtubs, door knobs, hinges, light fixtures, and closet systems. They sell to large hardware chains and to large building contractors in the Midwest. The company is located in Ohio. Stylex was founded in 1964 by George Stillwell.

They are now starting to advertise directly to individuals. They want to get the customer into hardware stores to buy their brand by name. The company has six million shares of stock. Stillwell kept fifty one percent of the stock (3,060,000). The company is not publicly traded. In 1979, Stillwell gave stock to the following; Joseph Everton received five percent, Stanley Horworth got five percent, Robert Cleary three percent, Albert Forman three percent, Beatrice Patterson and Dietmar Wertzer each got two and one half percent. At the same time, Stillwell gave stock bonuses to other employees who did not have stock. He gave one hundred shares to each employee that had three years working for the company. In addition, for each year they had worked for the company over the initial three year period, each employee was given another fifty shares. This practice has continued to the current year of 1986.

CHAPTER 1

Doris Wilcox, a thirty year old with short dark hair, stood in front of the fifteen executives of Stylex Custom Hardware Company and started her speech in a soft, but upbeat tone. "I am happy and excited to have been appointed as the Director of Marketing and Public Relations of Stylex Custom Hardware Company. I look forward to expanding – "

"Excuse me." Robert Cleary stood, a half smile on a handsome face, distinguished by a thin scar from his ear to his chin, his deep-set eyes reminiscent of an eagle searching for prey. "I am sorry to interrupt; no actually, I am not sorry to interrupt. I am Robert Cleary, Sales Manager. I have twenty two salesmen covering this state, Tennessee, and four other states. Wouldn't it be more advantageous to add six more salesmen so we can adequately cover our territory, knock on doors, and stand in front of our customers, eye-to-eye, to sell our products instead of spending money on ads that end up wrapped around garbage?"

Joseph Everton, CEO said, "Robert, take it easy..."

Doris held up her hand to stop Everton and said, "Please let me respond." She stood a little taller in her dark blue, and very conservative suit; her one hundred thirty pounds of well-proportioned body leaning a little bit forward poised for a fight, her words clipped, and the soft tone gone. "Mr. Cleary, the answer to your question is no, and I wish to emphasize that *no*."

Robert Cleary smiled and opened his mouth to speak but was quickly cut off by Doris, who continued. "The success of this company is a tribute to the excellent job being done by your salesmen, given the tools with which they have to work. I propose to accomplish three things. First, your salesmen will not have to knock at the door of our prospective customers. The door will be opened and they will be eagerly shown in by the purchaser. Second, when the salesman enters the customer's office, he will find our ad on the customer's desk and not in the garbage as you indicated. Third, and I am afraid the most difficult, I wish to reinvent the term salesman to salesperson,

1

convincing you that women are a major force in the home furnishing business. They can not only buy, but also sell the products manufactured by Stylex." The five females sitting in the room clapped loudly, joined half-heartedly by several of the men sitting next to them.

"I want to thank all of you in advance for your support, and I look forward to meeting with you individually to get your input on the direction Stylex should be moving," she concluded.

Robert Cleary, as he turned to leave the room, gave a sardonic smile and in a stage whisper said, "Good luck." Doris shot back, a little louder to overcome the murmurs, "Thank you for your support and open mindedness, Mr. Cleary." Robert looked back as he left the room, his smile gone. Later, as the meeting adjourned, a few of the men gave an unconvincing, "Welcome aboard," and a noncommittal smile. One exception was a six foot five giant who approached Doris, holding out his hand, and saying, "Sounds like you're going to be a welcome addition. I am Forman."

Doris extended her hand, which was immediately engulfed in the big man's hand and said, "Are you the foreman or are you Mr. Forman?"

"My name is Albert Forman. Nobody calls me Albert. They just call me Forman. And yes, I am the shop foreman." Albert continued to hold her hand as he went on, "I would like it if you would call me Albert. If you need anything at all from the Manufacturing Department, or if anyone gives you any trouble, just call me. I will take care of it." Forman then let go of her hand, turned, and walked out of the meeting.

George Stillwell, the, fifty eight year old President of Stylex, along with Joseph Everton, the CEO, then approached Doris, and with a slight smile said, "Well, Doris, I am amazed. You really made a hit with Forman. No one here calls Forman by his first name. A smarty once called him Albert and Forman slapped him hard enough to break his jaw. On the other hand, it looks like you picked your fight with Robert Cleary. Robert can be a little stiff necked and puts on a tough exterior. If you want, I'll talk to him."

"If you want, I could lend you a baseball bat so you can get his attention," Joseph Everton, the white haired and stocky fifty five year old CEO added.

2

"Oh, no," quickly interjected Doris, laughing, "If you talk to him it will just make him more intransigent. I'll just embarrass, cajole, humor, and enthrall him with my charm into doing what is best for the company." and with a smile added, "And doing what I want."

She continued, "However, I am certainly glad to have made a hit with Albert Forman. By the way he shook my hand, I can't believe he would be so violent! His handshake was so gentle. What's his background?"

"Oh, Forman," Stillwell said, "I grew up with Forman and I took him on when I started the company. He's a hell of a nice guy except for one thing. Don't cross him. He has a vicious temper and, at six foot five and two hundred and sixty pounds, can be very dangerous. He is exceptionally strong. We were moving some machinery when a portion fell on a workman's leg and crushed it. Forman lifted it so they could drag the man out. The machine weighed over eight hundred pounds. I've gotten him out of several bad scrapes. Three big guys attacked him. He beat the hell out of all three, and then they sued him for assault and battery. But, since he got into his sixties, he's been pretty mellow. Returning to Robert, I hope you can sweet-talk him over to your side. I'll just watch the battle. Good luck. If you need anything, just let me know." He turned and, along with Everton following, left the room.

Robin Taylor, Marketing Manager, joined the other women at the meeting. Deana Zimmer, Accounting Department Manager, and Brenda Vogel, Advertising Manager, were in their mid-thirties. Beatrice Patterson was a short fifty-something woman with a pretty face and a few too many pounds. They gathered around Doris, all with big smiles on their faces. Robin smiled at Doris, "Wow. You really made a hit with Forman. He's never spoken to me the whole time I've worked here."

Beatrice shook her head, the smile leaving her face, "Yeah, you're a first with Forman. However, Robert's another story. He's been top dog around here for quite a while. I'm sorry to say, he is going to fight you at every turn, until he makes you so miserable, you just leave. He's my nephew and I love him dearly, but he will fight you tooth and nail."

3

"Beatrice," Doris smiled, "if he wants a fight, he has come to the right place. I am even pretty good at karate. As long as management lets me, I am going to run my program, and I think it will be a success. Robert is going to hate me so much he'll think it's love." They all laughed. Brenda Vogel, the shortest of the group at five foot three inches, with short curly black hair, shot in with, "Yeah, he has been on my case every day for the past two years. Every time I come up with a set of ads, he chops them down to nothing and makes them so small you couldn't wrap garbage in them if you wanted to. You can imagine my relief that I'll now be reporting to you."

Robin Taylor, another black haired, five foot plus chimed in, "Me, too. Every marketing strategy I've come up with just doesn't fit what he wants, or as he likes to put it, it is just garbage."

Doris, laughing said, "He really likes garbage." They all laughed. Then, the smile gone, she looked at the women standing around her and started, "Now look, I'm going to ask a question you don't have to answer. I'm asking because I just want to know if there is anyone besides you all that I can look to for some support in what I want to accomplish?"

None of the women were smiling now and for a moment they were all silent. Deana, looking straight at Doris, while the others were looking everywhere else, said, "Some things in this place are a bit old school. If you notice, the senior management around here are all men. Some of them are not happy at all when a woman is in a position with any kind of power. Some of them will never support you because of that."

Doris looked thoughtful. Deana then said, "It might help if you knew about personal relationships that could affect your interactions. So the question is, are any of us involved with the guys here? Well the answer, for me, is yes. I don't know how the others feel about talking, but I am heavily involved with the Production Manager, Dietmar Wertzer. He's a straight-up guy, and I'm positive he would not go out of his way to create trouble for you. On the other hand, he will not go against Robert Cleary."

Beatrice Patterson smiled, "I've got to get back to work. By the way, call me Bea, everyone does. I'd love to talk with you later, Doris." With that, she left.

Brenda said, "Robin and I are really looking forward to working with you," and pulled Robin away.

Doris called after them as they were leaving the room, "Brenda, let's meet tomorrow at eleven in your office. I'll give you a quick outline of the direction I want to go in and, at the same time, go over your ideas." There was quick agreement from Brenda, and they were gone.

Doris looked around the empty room, smiled, and said aloud to no one, "Well, here comes the fight of my life." She left the room and headed for her office, slowly shaking her head.

Doris entered through the door leading to the Advertising and Marketing Department and up to a desk with a nameplate on the edge that read, Alice Donald. Arranged behind her were three doors. The center door was labeled Doris Wilcox, Director, Marketing and Public Relations. The left door was labeled Robin Taylor, Assistant Marketing Manager, and on the right the door was labeled Brenda Vogel, Assistant Advertising Manager. Alice Donald acted as secretary for the group. Doris stopped in front of Alice's desk. "Alice", she started, "We have our job cut out for us. I will be giving you a lot of dictation and discussing a lot of my plans with Robin and Brenda. At times I may speak rather bluntly and, I am afraid, not complimentary. I expect what is discussed here to remain here."

Looking very serious, Alice said "Of course, Mrs. Wilcox."

"Oh, Alice," Doris interrupted, "Please call me Doris."

"Thank you, Doris," Alice continued, "As you probably know, I have only been here three months. I am married to an electrician who works for the city. My mother lives with us and takes care of our little girl. My allegiance is to you and this department."

Doris nodded, "Thanks for giving me your history. We will get along fine, I'm sure." With that, she went into her office and sat down in her chair. Leaning back, she closed her eyes and gave a big sigh, "Well, here goes nothing." She leaned forward, picked up the phone, and checking her phone list, dialed. In the middle of the first ring a voice curtly announced, "Stanley H..."

"Stanley," Doris talked into the phone, "this is Doris."

5

"Oh, yes," Stanley came back in a much softer tone. "How can I help you today?"

Doris relaxed a little and said, "First, do I call you Stanley or Stanley H.?"

Stanley laughed, "Well, with me and Stanley Woo here, we sometimes confuse people. We do the H and W to avoid confusion. So the answer is, Stanley is fine."

"Sounds good," continued Doris, "I will be needing a bunch of financial information, and I wanted to know if you wanted me to go through you or through Deana."

"Well," Stanley said, "I will be glad to help, but if you ask me, I will only have to ask Deana. So, how about I tell Deana to give you what you want. You'll get it a lot faster."

"Stanley," Doris, now relaxed, said, "I really appreciate your cooperation."

"Listen, Doris," he said, "not everyone here hates you."

Doris laughed out loud. "Stanley, I guess if you ever hate me I'll know it."

At this Stanley said, "I doubt it will ever happen, but if it does you will be the first to know! I'll call Deana now and she will give you whatever you need."

"Thanks, Stanley H." Doris said, and hung up the phone. "Well," she said to the room, "that wasn't so bad."

The door to the office opened, Alice stuck her head in, "Did you call me?"

"No, I was just talking to myself. I do that a lot." Doris got up, crossed to Alice and asked, "Where is Deana's office?"

Alice, a surprised look on her face asked, "Is there anything I can get from Deana and bring to you?"

"Not this time," Doris answered, "I'm not yet sure what I want."

Alice walked to the outer door with Doris following her and said, "The quick way is down the hall to the stairs, one flight up, turn to your left, and you're facing Deana's office."

Doris nodded, walked to the stairs, went up one flight, and turned left. She faced the door marked Deana Zimmer. Doris took two steps toward the door when someone said, "I guess the ad campaign is already done that will double Stylex sales!"

Without turning, Doris said, "Of course, Robert, the ad campaign is at the printers. Check the Sunday papers." Doris then turned, took a step toward Robert Cleary and continued. "I am sure you're going to be thrilled with the campaign and the results."

"What?" Robert Cleary said, "Listen, the way we do things around here is, we discuss these plans and get input from people with experience. We just don't go off half assed."

"Robert," Doris said in a surprised voice, "Such language. You are offending my delicate little ears. Just for that I am going to cancel the ads right now and wait until I get input." She turned, took two steps and said "Have someone with such experience call Alice for a three o'clock appointment. The ads will run with the input I get at that time."

Robert under his breath said, "Wise ass."

"I heard that," Doris said and opened the door marked Accounting. She crossed the threshold and closed the door, leaving Robert standing in the hallway.

She entered a large office divided into glass cubicles on each side of a central aisle. The cubicles were marked Accounts Receivable, Accounts Payable, General Ledger, and Manager. She smiled at the heads looking up as she passed to the manager's cubicle. Deana looked up, motioned "come in" with her hand and waited for Doris to enter. She smiled "You've hit the ground running. Stanley called and said to give you whatever you want."

Doris answered, "Did he tell you how I can get Robert Cleary off my back? I haven't done anything yet and he wants to sensor it."

Deana gave a short laugh and said, "Get used to it. You're going to be sleeping with him from now on."

7

Doris raised her eyebrows and said, "I hope you mean that metaphorically." They both started laughing. In between laughs Deana said, "Doris, I am really going to enjoy working with you."

Doris stopped laughing and continued, "Deana, thanks for that and for being so open with me this morning. I will try to be as little a pain in the ass as possible, but I figured the best way to get the inside workings of Stylex are through the financials. I would like quarterly financial statements for the last two years, 1984 and 1985, and the quarterly financials for the first two quarters of this year. I would also like aged accounts receivable for the same quarters. Do you have quarterly sales figures for each product?"

Deana opened her mouth to speak, closed it, opened it again and answered, "Yes…Wow, if I didn't know better, I'd say your gunning for the old man's job."

Doris answered back, "By the old man, do you mean Everton or Stillwell?"

"Stillwell," Deana answered, "Everton is only fifty five."

"Well," Doris lowered her voice, "what's wrong with a woman heading up Stylex? Maybe we can show them what hardware a woman wants in the home, from doorknobs, to cabinets, to closet units."

Deana, nodding her head up and down, responded, "I'll start sending what you want to your desk in the morning. Oh, and when you become President, I want to be CFO. I've got some ideas to streamline this department. Every time I suggest something they tell me to keep to the books. Stanley is a great guy but he wants to do things the old fashioned way. He is just too laid back. He says he wants to retire in two years and Brenton is licking his chops waiting to get into that chair. And when he does, I think I'm history."

"Oh, what's with this Brenton Lazarus?" Doris asked. "When we met, he wouldn't even look at me. He already seems to hate me."

"Well," Deana answered, "I don't like to say bad things about someone I really don't like, but he really is a creep. The only people he talks to nicely are Stillwell and Everton, and barely to them. He treats everyone like shit, particularly women, and for some reason has Carmen, outside, terrified. I cannot find out why. But, believe me, it's something real bad."

"I'm glad it's not just me." Doris said, "I guess we will have to watch out for Brenton Lazarus." Getting up to walk to the door, she said, "Well, thanks for your help. Let's go up the ladder together," and left.

"Wait, Doris," Deana called as she got up, "let me introduce you to the girls that do all the work." She walked into the hall with Doris. "Listen up, ladies," she said, "I would like you to meet Doris Wilcox. You all have heard about her joining Stylex. Hopefully, she will help get us out of our male dominated environment. Doris, this is Susan Butler, Accounts Receivable, Carmen Mendez, Accounts Payable and Payroll, and Frances Pestic, General Ledger." The three girls nodded their hellos.

Doris smiled and said, "Nice to meet you. I hope I won't cause you too much additional work, and yes, I intend to make us women much more than, 'the other human beings'."

Susan and Frances laughed; Carmen smiled, nodded, and sat back down at her desk.

"Thanks again, Deana," Doris said, "Do you want me to stop by tomorrow to pick up the financials?"

"No," answered Deana, "When I get the info together, I'll bring it down to your office."

Doris nodded and left the office. When she got into the hall, Forman was standing a few doors down. He smiled, turned, and walked away. Doris called after him, "Hello, Albert, how are you?"

Forman just raised his arm above his head and waved his hand in answer. Doris shook her head, shrugged her shoulders, and went the opposite way, down the hall, to the stairway, down to her office.

Back in Accounting, Deana turned to the group and explained what Doris wanted. "When you get the stuff together put it on my desk. I'll be out the rest of the day. I'll pick it up in the morning and take it down to Doris." They nodded and Deana left the office.

Carmen in a sullen tone said, "Why does she want all this information? She is in marketing, not finance and accounting. What is she planning to do? Run the company?"

"Who cares," Susan shot back, "we can't be treated any worse."

"Yeah," Frances added, "Woo treats us like servants; not equals and Lazarus is no better." At the mention of Lazarus' name Carmen paled, lowered her head, and stared back at the papers on which she was working.

***

From down the hall, Robert saw Doris returning back to her department. He stood, shook his head and walked to the stairs going down to the next floor. He walked past the door marked Marketing and Advertising, on to the next door marked Sales Manager, and entered.

Bea, sitting at her desk, looked up and smiled, "What's that big frown on your face for?"

"That woman," he snorted, "She is going to be a real pain in the ass. I don't know how a person could work with that… that opinionated *bitch*!"

"Robert," Bea smiled up at him, "Whomever are you talking about?"

"You know damn well who I am talking about. She is going to be as bad to work with as you are. I don't know why I don't fire your ass out of here, anyway."

Bea, her smile gone now, slapped her hand on the desk and spoke in a low threatening voice, "Robert, don't you ever speak to me like that again. I still have that paddle I used on you when you were a sassy little kid, and I will beat you within an inch of your life if you ever speak like that again."

"Oh, Aunt Bea, I'm sorry. That woman is going to drive me to drink, and I think pretty fast. Besides, I couldn't fire you if I wanted to, not with you living with the boss for the past two years. Why don't you marry him, anyway? He's been asking you for a year now. Stanley is a hell of a nice guy. He's one of the few around here that has his head screwed on right."

"Robert, I tried that twice," Bea said, leaning back in her chair, a soft and sad look on her face. "Each time I thought it was the right one. The first wanted to use me as a punching bag. That only happened once before I threw him out. The other one wanted to go to bed with

10

anything that wore a skirt. Maybe if I just live with this one, he will stay focused on the relationship."

"Well," Robert said, "I guess you know best. Let me know when it's three fifteen or three thirty. I have a three o'clock meeting with that woman to approve ads."

"Don't you want me to let you know a few minutes before three so you can go next door for your meeting? Did she ask you to approve her ads?" Bea asked, a smile back on her face.

"I don't want to be too early for the meeting. And someone has got to tell her what to do. Just let me know a little after three." Robert said as he walked into his office, a smug grin on his face.

At three fifteen Robert walked over to Advertising and Marketing. He nodded at Alice, walked to Doris Wilcox's office, and without knocking, opened the door. He walked up to the chair in front of Doris's desk and sat down. Alice was at the door and said, "I'm sorry, Doris."

Doris held up her hand, "It's OK, Alice." and turning to Robert said, "Come in, Robert, please have a seat."

"What about those ads you want me to approve?" Robert said in response to Doris's remark.

"Ads, Robert? I don't want you to approve any ads. The input meeting was at three and it's all over." Doris smiled and sat back looking at Robert, who stared back at her. They looked at each other for a full minute before Doris leaned forward, no longer smiling.

"OK," She said, "by now, I hope some of this has sunk into your little head. First, you are no longer head of Advertising and Marketing. I'm going to let you spend all your energy on running the Sales Department. When I get an advertising and marketing campaign set up, it will be presented to upper management. Do you understand the adjective, 'upper'? The heads of Accounting, Production, Sales, Legal, and New Products will be asked to make suggestions. I emphasize the word *suggestions*. Now, when and if I come to see you, I will knock on your door and wait to be invited in. I expect the same courtesy from you. Do you have any questions?"

11

Robert got up, went to the door, opened it, turned back, and said "Not now." He was gone, leaving the door open.

Alice, Brenda, and Robin stood in the open door and Robin said, "Doris, we all just love you."

Doris laughed, "I didn't realize I was talking loud enough for everyone to hear." They all laughed and walked back to their desks.

At five o'clock Brenda came to Doris' open office door, tapped on the door, and said, "Doris, we can't take any more excitement today. If you don't need anything else, we're heading out."

Doris looked up. "Oh, go ahead," She laughed, "I'm right behind you." She closed the pad in front of her, put it into a drawer, locked it, and picked up her bag. *"Well,"* She thought, *"This is the first day of the rest of my time on this job. I hope there are many more days to come."*

When she got out to the parking lot it was almost empty. She didn't notice Albert Forman standing up against the building wall across from where she parked, watching her as she approached her car. The bulk of the plant workers worked from seven in the morning until four in the afternoon. She unlocked her car, got in, gave a long sigh, started the car, and said, "First day at Stylex is over."

CHAPTER 2

At five minutes to nine A.M., Deana walked into the Accounting Department said good morning to Carmen, the only one there, and walked into her office. Brenton Lazarus sat in front of her desk, a pile of papers on his lap. At thirty five, athletically built with a handsome dark complexioned face, this man did not exude friendliness.

"How are you this morning?" She asked.

"Never mind the pleasantries. What are these?" He growled, holding up the papers from his lap. The growl seemed to be his normal tone of voice, unless he was talking to Stillwell or Everton.

"Why, I have no idea what those papers are, Brenton," Deana replied, an amused look on her face. "Why don't you tell me what they are?"

"You know damn well what they are. They are the financials for two and a half years; aged accounts receivables, and payables. Do you think you are going to give them to that new woman?"

Deana smiled, "That new woman, Brenton? Who on earth do you mean?" all the while looking him straight in the eye thinking, "*You asshole, say her name. Yeah, and in two years you won't be assistant CEO, you'll be out on your butt.*"

Brenton jumped up and snarled at her, "You know who I mean. That mistake they made Director of Marketing Department. I understand she can't even keep a husband."

"Why, Brenton," Deana said softly, settling back in her chair, her eyes narrowed, her mouth a straight line, "Aren't you divorced?" She continued, "Please put those papers back on my desk. Stanley, my boss, the CFO, told me to give them to that mistake."

Brenton, his eyes bulging in anger, hissed, "We'll see about this. That damn Stanley is an old fool." Clutching the packet of papers to his chest, he turned and stormed out, slamming the door behind him.

Deana walked out of her office. Susan and Frances sat, mouths half open, looking scared. Carmen sat with her eyes lowered.

"Alright," Deana said, as she looked each one in the eye. "I don't know how that asshole found out about the papers on my desk, but I want a duplicate of those financials and accounts receivable. Carmen, I want a list of accounts payable at every quarter end for 1984 and 1985, and I want a list of payables as of the end of the second week of the month, and the month end for each month this year."

"I can't do that," stuttered Carmen.

Deana took a step toward Carmen and in a stage whisper said, "Do it." Raising her voice again she continued, "I want them now and if shit-head returns tell him I'm with Stanley H.!" With that she walked out the door, slamming it behind her.

Susan and Frances started opening file drawers, taking out files, slamming file cabinets, taking turns at the copy machine, all the while Susan murmuring, "The shit is going to hit the fan today. Shit is going to hit the fan today."

Frances looked over at Carmen and snapped, "Carmen, get off your ass and start doing what you are supposed to be doing."

Carmen slowly rose, opened a file cabinet drawer and took out some files, all the while whispering, "I can't do this. What am I going to do? Oh Jesus, please protect my family."

"What are you saying, Carmen?" Frances asked, looking at her, "What is the matter with you? We do as we are told. Nothing is going to happen to you."

Carmen looked at Frances, tears running down her cheeks, and said, "My family is going to die if Mr. Lazarus finds out I gave this information to Mrs. Wilcox."

"What are you talking about?" Frances asked as Susan turned from the copy machine to look at Carmen. "What has Lazarus got on you that makes you so afraid of him?"

"Never mind," Carmen said, "I will get the papers ready." And with that, she turned her back on Frances and Susan and started assembling files.

There was no friendly chitchat as they worked feverishly to complete their tasks. Susan and Frances kept looking over at Carmen and then at each other, shaking their heads, watching Carmen move like a zombie as she completed her work.

Meanwhile, Deana marched down the hall, eyes narrowed, breathing in short controlled exhalations and muttering, "I'll fix you, you asshole, I'll fix you, you asshole," over and over. She passed the elevator, shoving open the door to the stairwell with such force it hit the wall and bounced back almost knocking her down. She slammed it again, just as hard, this time stepping out of the way as it bounced back, and started up the stairs two at a time. Her skirt stretched and rode up past her knees as her legs rose to take the two step gait she was using to get up the two floors. Reaching the top, she grabbed the door handle, swung it open and quickly stepped through before it hit her as it bounced back. She turned and stopped at the door marked Stanley Horworth, Chief Financial Officer. She knocked, opened the door, and walked into the office.

Stanley, sitting at his desk with a pile of papers in front of him, looked up, eyes widening, "What is wrong, Deana? You have smoke coming out of both ears!" He said. "Did I do something wrong? I hate when you yell at me," and laughed.

Deana couldn't stop her lips curling up in a grin, but it quickly disappeared. She leaned over the desk putting her face close to Stanley's.

"Stanley, I am too mad to laugh. That son of a bitch Lazarus just came into my office and took the papers I was going to give Doris right off my desk. Do I give them to her, or don't I give them to her?"

"Oh my, he is getting to be a pain," Stanley said as he leaned back in his chair. "You give them to her. I'll talk to Brenton Lazarus. Try not to get so upset."

Deana straightened up. "I'm sorry, Stanley, but he pushes every one of my wrong buttons. You know when he gets Joe's job I'll be the first to get booted."

Stanley laughed. "I'll tell you what, before Joe leaves I'll work out something to protect you. Now go get a cup of coffee and relax a bit. It's not good to get so upset."

"OK," Deana said, her face showing surprise about what he had said about protecting her. "I'll do your coffee therapy. Thanks for the

15

kind words, Stanley." Deana turned and left the office a smile on her face. "Alright, Lazarus, one for my side," she whispered and thought, *"What did Stanley mean when he said he would protect me?"*

After Deana entered the stairwell to the stairs back to her office, the elevator door opened and Lazarus walked past Stanley H.'s office and into Everton's, ignoring Alice. Everton's secretary was sitting in the outer office. He walked to the inner office's closed door, opened it, entered, and slapped the bundle of papers on Everton's desk. He stood looking at him breathing heavily.

"Brenton," Everton said in a soft voice, "Is there anything wrong? You look very upset."

"Damn it, Joe, Stanley H. just gave that Wilcox woman all the Stylex financial information for two years. I know you don't think it's important, but I just don't trust the bitch. She is supposed to be making ads, not doing a financial analysis of Stylex."

Everton leaned forward, "Relax, Brenton, relax. You are under too much pressure. You're trying to do all your work and mine. Since you took over inventory control, you're trying to be all over the plant floor. The Wilcox woman wants to learn what we are selling and to whom. Our competition probably knows as much about Stylex as we do. I think it's time for you to relax a little. Get Deana and her girls to handle inventory control."

"No, no, Joe, I enjoy that job. It's no big deal. Let's just forget this thing about the Wilcox woman. I'll give Deana back the papers." With that Brenton picked up the papers and walked out.

Grace stuck her head in the door and asked, "Is he OK?"

"I think so." Everton said. "I hope he doesn't have a nervous breakdown."

Grace laughed, "He's too mean to have a breakdown," and walked out the door.

***

It was a quiet day for Doris. She had not heard about the early confrontation between Deana and Brenton. She spent the morning looking over past ads and the ads of their few competitors. She called in Robin and Brenda and they discussed the print ads and the

16

possibility of going on television to bring Stylex up to speed in the advertising game. At noon they went down to the cafeteria. As they entered, they saw Forman standing near the door. When he saw Doris he waved hello and left the dining room.

"Everywhere I go I seem to be running into Albert. I almost get the feeling he is following me. It's kind of scary," Doris said.

"Oh, just get used to it. He's all over the place. I wouldn't worry," answered Brenda.

CHAPTER 3

The next afternoon Robert Cleary walked into Beatrice's office with a big smile on his face and started, "Hello, Aunt Bea, how are you today?"

Beatrice looked up. "What do you want Robert? I'm busy doing your work."

"Who said I wanted anything," Robert said, the smile still frozen on his face, "How are you today?"

"Please, Robert," Beatrice exhaled, "You stopped calling me *Aunt* Bea when you were six years old, unless, of course, you wanted something. Now, what do you want?"

"I don't want anything, Bea," Robert said. "I just want to find out about that Wilcox woman's credentials. I want to find out if she knows what she is doing. What can you tell me about her anyway?" Robert asked, the smile still plastered on his face.

"The Wilcox woman?" Bea said, "Let me get her file." Bea stood up and went to the file cabinet behind her. With the key that hung around her neck, she unlocked the drawers, opened and closed two of them, relocked the cabinet, and sat back down in her chair. She sat looking at Robert for a long pause and then said, "Oh, I just remembered, I can't find her file. You can come back next week when I find her file or, better still, if you want to know all about her, I know where all the information is. Go ask her. Now go sit at your desk and do your work."

"Gee whiz, Bea, why are you so testy? I just wanted some information," Robert said, looking slightly uncomfortable.

"Robert, you know I love you dearly," Bea said continuing, "but, you know what? I think I am on that Wilcox woman's side, that is, for the time being. Let's leave her alone for a while and see what she can do. I'll be watching you, so behave."

Robert turned to leave, and said, "Well, so much for family."

Bea shot back, "Just remember that this family is watching you." The door closed and Bea thought to herself, *"Robert, I think you are in for a big fight."* Bea answered her ringing phone a few moments later, "Bea Patterson here." The voice on the phone said, "Bea, you want to eat out tonight or at home?"

"Stanley," she answered, "let's eat out, I don't feel like cooking or making you clean up."

Stanley laughed, "I'm for that. What about the Crabcake House? I'm in the mood for fish."

"I'll meet you there at six, Stan," Beatrice said, hanging up the phone, and leaning back. *"We have been going together for two years and living together for one, and I am still afraid to marry you. I don't know what's wrong with me,"* she thought.

***

At six o'clock, Stanley H. pulled into the Crabcake House parking lot in his Honda Accord, followed by Beatrice in her Ford 4 X 4 truck. Stanley waited by his car as Beatrice disembarked from her truck. "Bea, I say this every day to myself and a lot of times to you, but, aside from the rednecks, what is your reason for driving that huge, gas guzzling monster?"

"I know, I know," Bea said, "but I love the looks I get from the rednecks when they see a little old lady get out of the monster truck. I really love the power. I think it's turned into a status symbol for me. It tells me I can do anything I want."

"You don't need a truck to tell you that. I tell you that all the time." Stanley laughed.

They entered the restaurant and were warmly greeted by the owner who said, "Usual table, folks?" Stanley nodded and they were led to a small table at the back of the restaurant, with menus placed in front of them.

Stanley said, "I know what I want: crab cakes, bleu cheese dressing on the salad, fries, and coffee."

Beatrice added, "I'll have the same thing and water with lemon."

After the manager left, Stanley looked at Beatrice and shook his head. "I don't know what to think about Brenton. I told Deana to give Doris some financial information, and he went bonkers. He took the papers away from Deana and went screaming to Joe. He seems to be getting paranoid. He thinks Doris is some kind of spy trying to get information for our competition. Joe said he quieted him down a bit. What do you think is wrong with him?"

"You know I don't like him. You know I don't trust him. I think he would kill Joe for his job, if he felt he could get away with it. There is also something going on between him and Carmen Mendez. I don't know what it is, but it is not good."

"You mean Carmen in the Accounting Department? Are they going out together or something?" Stanley asked.

"You mean, are they doing what we are doing?" Beatrice asked.

"If you would marry me, than we wouldn't be doing what we are doing. If you don't want to marry me, why do you stay with me?" Stanley said, "And don't give me that, 'I don't know,' answer. We've been together two years. Everyone knows we are a couple. It's just that we are getting old, and two old people fooling around is boring."

"What do you mean 'boring', Stanley? How would you like to eat supper alone? Boring! Well? What do you mean 'boring'?" Beatrice said, sitting straight in her chair, looking Stanley straight in the eye.

"Hold it, hold it, hold it," Stanley said, "I didn't say we were boring. I said…" Then he started laughing, seeing the smile on Bea's face. "You always do that to me. You get that scary look, and I think I am in the doghouse. You are still avoiding the question. Bea, I love you. I want to spend the rest of my life with you, what little there is remaining. You don't have to work. We can travel. We can do anything we want."

Bea looked at him and shook her head. "Stanley, I love you with all my heart. You know I don't have to work. The property out west that my father left my brother and his kids throws off enough money to keep the whole family very comfortable. Robert's income from the ranch out there is enough to keep him and the girls living in style for the rest of his life. Anna also has the money from her late husband. Robert works because he enjoys what he does, and so do I. What am I going to do with you when you retire? The way it is now, I can keep an eye on you. I worry if I marry you, you will feel stuck and will want to get away from me. I don't know if I could take another divorce. Anyway, why aren't you out looking for a beautiful, young thing? You are handsome, charming, and rich. You could have anyone you want."

"Bea." Stanley reached across the table and took her hand, "First, I did look for a beautiful young thing; it's you. Second, if you don't want to quit work, then fine, I won't quit work. I will sign a prenuptial agreement so I won't get your fabulous wealth. And…"

Beatrice interrupted him, "Does that mean that I can't have *your* fabulous wealth?"

"You know you get to share my wealth whether you marry me or not," he said.

"Share your wealth, Stanley? I didn't know you had any relatives that were going to share your vast wealth with me. Have you got a wife, or is it a girlfriend you're not telling me about?"

"Would you marry me if my girlfriend or wife said it was fine?" Stanley said, and seeing the look on her face continued, "Oh, Bea, I don't have a wife, and I don't have a girlfriend. That is, except for you, and I don't want you to be my girlfriend any longer. I want you to be my wife. And when you are my wife, you can see my will and approve of anyone that is going to share my vast wealth."

"Damn it, Stanley, I am going to marry you. But, I'll tell you what. The next time we go out to dinner, I will wait for you to ask me again. *Then,* I will say yes. If you change your mind, you had better not ask me again because you'll really be stuck. Am I clear?"

Stanley sat with his mouth slightly opened as if to speak, then got up, walked around the table, leaned over, and kissed Bea. People at nearby tables were looking as Stanley straightened. He looked around, smiled, and announced, "Ladies and gentlemen, I am going to marry this young lady."

There was polite applause. Bea, with a red face, said, "Stanley, please sit down. You are embarrassing me. Please remember, you have a get out of jail card. All you have to do is not ask me to marry you."

21

Stanley again bent down and gave her a long kiss. He straightened up and said, "You know, you have made me the happiest man in the world. Now seriously, are Carmen and Lazarus going out or something?"

"I don't think it's that." Beatrice started, "Deana tells me, every time his name is mentioned, Carmen starts shaking. I checked her file. She is not married, has a six year old girl, and a boy that I think is about four. She is a naturalized citizen, both kids born here. Her mother and her brother are listed as living with her. I think she is the sole support for the family. I think the brother mows lawns and does yard work. I don't know under what status they are here."

"Bea," Stanley said, "nose around a little. I don't want to talk to Brenton; it may cause more trouble for her, if there is any. See what Deana can find out. Maybe we can give Carmen's brother a job."

"That's a good idea," Bea said, looking thoughtful. "You know what," she continued, "I just had a fantastic idea. What about a day care center? We could hire Carmen's mother, and maybe Anna would be interested in heading it up."

Stanley looking surprised said, "You mean have Anna bring Robert's kids to Stylex, and have everyone else bring their kids too? We could end up with fifty kids or more. The insurance costs would be astronomical. I think I like the other idea better."

"What idea is that?" Bea asked.

"Giving Carmen's brother a job, "Stanley answered, "It's clean, simple, and doesn't have fifty screaming kids around. Anyway, George has come up with some crazy ideas he wants me to check out, so let's hold off on any more crazy changes around Stylex for the time being."

"Crazy ideas sound more interesting." Beatrice said, "Tell me more."

Before Stanley could answer, the waiter approached, put their dinner plates in front of them and said, "I'll check back with you in a few minutes. If you need anything, just holler," and left them alone again.

"Thanks," Stanley called after him and picking up his fork started to fill it with food.

"Wait a minute," Bea said, "what about the crazy ideas?"

"Enough business for one night, eat before it gets cold." Stanley smiled and started to eat.

"Stanley, are you going to leave me hanging? What ideas? I hate when you start a subject and just clam up." Bea said in an exasperated voice.

"Bea, you're right. It's clam time. Let's talk later." Stanley, smiling, put a fork full of food in his mouth.

CHAPTER 4

Stanley Woo walked into Stanley Horworth's office. He sat down and leaned back in his chair.

Stanley H., watched, and waited, but Woo just sat there looking at him without speaking. Finally Stanley H. said, "Good afternoon, Woo, is there anything you want to talk about?"

"I've been going over the figures for the last four years," Woo began, "Sales have increased seven and a quarter percent average but profits have only increased an average of three quarters of one percent to three percent."

"That's not so bad, Woo," Stanley H. said. "Everybody's making money, and Stillwell keeps giving generous bonuses to the employees."

Woo leaned forward answering, "It's easy for Stillwell. He's got millions. Listen, H," Woo continued, "I'm not talking about throwing the workers out with nothing. We could give them 12 months pay as severance and some of the older ones two years pay. Without social security costs, pension benefits, and those damn bonuses we could probably triple our profits."

"Like you said, Woo," Stanley H. replied, "Stillwell has all the money in the world. He's not interested in making more. Anyway, we are all getting generous bonuses. We are making more here than we could make any place else."

Woo, a look of desperation on his face continued, "Look, he's not going to live forever. None of his family is interested in this business. Hell, Stillwell is not even interested in this business. What does he think will happen when he dies? His loveable employees will end up with nothing. And another thing, we're leaving opportunities for competition to come in and kill our business. With overseas labor, we could afford to drop our prices when any one tries to compete with us. We could kill them before they got a foothold. Moving production overseas is a win-win situation for everyone."

Stanley H. leaned forward, put his arms on his desk, exhaled, and said, "What about our little union? Are they going to support losing their jobs?"

Now Woo leaned back in his chair, smiled, and said, "Don't worry about our little union. I have already sounded Bill Bernard out on this, and he will go along. He will explain to the production staff that they cannot stop production moving overseas sooner or later. He will tell the workers that, if they cooperate, they can probably get one or two years pay up front. They will cooperate, especially when no pay is the alternative."

"I don't know, Woo," Stanley H. said, "You seem to have all the answers. I'll see what George has to say, but I don't think it will go over that easy. Maybe next week we can have a meeting with Bernard and see how many of the production staff will go along with the move. We certainly don't want a work stoppage now." Woo got up, moved to the door and said, "You'll see Stanley; this is the right thing to do. I'll tell Bernard you want to see him next week. He'll tell you how the employees feel. He'll tell you there will be no trouble." Woo opened the door, said, "See you later," and left.

Two minutes later Woo was sitting in Lazarus' office.

"Well, Woo, what's wrong?" Lazarus asked.

"I had to tell H about Bernard saying there will be no union problem about moving overseas." Woo continued, "He said he will talk to George, but wants to talk to Bernard. We have to make sure Bernard is on our side."

"Why the hell did you bring Bernard up? Now we definitely have to get him on our side before H gets hold of him. Get out of here and let me think." Lazarus said.

Woo got up and, without saying a word, left. Lazarus picked up the phone, dialed three numbers, and the phone was answered, "Accounting Department, Carmen speaking."

Lazarus said, "I want to know Bill Bernard's salary and bonus last year and his annual salary this year," and hung up the phone.

Carmen put the receiver down, got up and went to the file drawer, and pulled out the file marked Bill Bernard. She went back to her desk. She opened the file, picked up the phone, and dialed three numbers. When Lazarus answered the phone she said, "Twenty eight thousand five hundred dollars, thirteen thousand dollars, thirty one thousand dollars," and hung up the phone.

Lazarus put down the phone and looked at the three numbers Carmen gave him. Thirty one thousand plus a probable fifteen thousand bonus gives forty six thousand. Seventy five thousand per year, plus thirty thousand living expenses, plus twenty five thousand bonus, and a five year contract should do it. His mind made up, Lazarus dialed three numbers. When Woo answered the phone he said, "I want you and Bill Bernard at my place tomorrow, you at six thirty, and him at seven. And be on time."

"I'll be there." Woo said and both phones were hung up.

The Accounting Department phone rang again. Francis picked up the phone on the first ring, "Accounting Department, Frances speaking." The voice barked back, "Carmen!" Francis smiling asked, "Who's calling please?" She waited for Lazarus to start screaming. And Lazarus did scream, "Put her on the phone, damn it."

Frances pushed the hold button and said, "Carmen, for you, the asshole again."

Carmen paled, picked up the phone and said, "Yes, Sir?"

Without any introduction the voice barked, "Be there, at six o'clock." and the phone went dead. Susan and Frances were both looking at Carmen, who put down the phone and sat, with eyes lowered, slowly pulling pages out of files for copying.

Susan put her hands on her hips, and in a staccato voice said, "Carmen, what does he want with you?"

Carmen looked up in a panic; "Nothing, nothing, leave me alone." She then bent her head down over her work and kept pulling pages out of her files.

Susan and Frances looked at each other, and both, at the same time, shrugged their shoulders and shook their heads.

A few minutes later Carmen stopped, picked up her phone, and dialed a number. When the phone was answered she said, "I'll be home late tonight." and, without saying another word, hung up the phone.

CHAPTER 5

Doris pulled her car into the driveway of a light blue one-story frame house with a white picket fence along the front of the house. *"If everything goes well, I will buy this house. Three bedrooms, two baths, and a really nice neighborhood makes this perfect; a perfect place. Unless, of course, I meet another Mr. Right,"* she thought. *"Frank Wilcox, why did you have to die on me? We were perfect. Our whole family was perfect, and you let that kid crash your plane. All that combat and not a scratch. One training mission and it's all over."*

She wiped the tears from her eyes, got out of the car, pushed the lock button, and went to the front door. She unlocked the door, opened it and yelled, "I'm home."

Immediately two squeaky voices calling "Mama! Mama!" sounded through the house, and two little girls ran to greet Doris. Doris bent, heaved both girls up in her arms, kissed each one on their, cheeks and set them down. "Mary, Susan," Doris gasped, "You're both definitely too big for me to hold. When did you get so big?"

Both girls laughed, and Mary Wilcox, Doris' six year old daughter said, "Come inside, Mama, Margaret has supper all ready." Susan, Doris' three year old daughter, still clinging to Doris' dress said, "Yes, supper ready." Doris and the girls entered the small dining room; the table in the middle of the room was set for four.

Margaret, a twenty three year old, dark complexioned girl came into the room carrying a big bowl of salad. She sat it on the table and said, "Salad first, then spaghetti with meat sauce and then, if you eat all your food, chocolate cake and milk for dessert."

Doris smiled; "At this rate, I'll need a new wardrobe. And why are we avoiding how you did on your accounting midterm?"

"Well," Margaret said, "with all that moaning and groaning I'm embarrassed to tell you. I got an 'A'."

"That is so fantastic, Margaret! I guess the late nights have paid off."

"Well," Margaret said, "a lot of the credit goes to you. You're giving me room, board, and a salary for just watching the kids after school and day care and for making supper for all of us. It has given me plenty of time to study instead of working all day, going to school at night, and then trying to study. And being with the girls has really been a joy. Now, girls, tell Mama what you did today."

Mary looked at Doris and began, "Well, we played games all day, and I have a best friend, and her name is Mary just like mine, and she is six years old just like me, and she has a sister just like me, and we're best friends."

"Wow, what an exciting day," exclaimed Doris laughing, "playing games and having a best friend with the same name. What is this Mary's last name?"

Mary shrugged her shoulders and said, "I don't know."

Margaret interrupted, "Their last name is Maxwell. I met Anna Maxwell, their Aunt. She picks up the girls and watches them for her brother, Bobby. He's a salesman, travels a lot, and keeps irregular hours. Mary's sister's name is Joan, and believe it or not, she is in Susan's nursery school class."

Susan stopped eating her salad and said "We played all day and Joan and me shared a mat for nap time. Joan is my best friend, too."

Doris and Margaret were laughing when Mary said, "Aunt Anna asked if we could come over after school and play."

Doris looking a little surprised asked, "What is this Aunt Anna?" and looked at Margaret.

"Oh," Margaret said, "Anna asked the girls to call her Aunt Anna. She said everyone does, and Maxwell is too long a name for the kids to remember. She asked me if I could bring the girls over for a play date this Tuesday. Anna would like for all of us to stay for supper. I told Anna I couldn't make supper on Tuesday because I have a study group I have to go to. I also told her I would ask you if it would be alright, and that I'd let her know if you would be joining them for supper. I'd stay here with the girls until you got home, of course."

"That will be great," Doris said, "tell Anna I'll bring an apple pie for dessert."

The rest of the meal was spent with Mary deciding what toys to take on the play date and with Susan mimicking each toy with one of hers. Doris and Margaret kept reminding the girls to "eat your food."

***

At six o'clock that evening the doorbell rang at 1524 S. W. 3rd Street, Apartment 12. Brenton Lazarus opened the door to Carmen standing in front of him. Without a word, he backed up and Carmen entered the apartment and closed the door. Walking back into his living room he said, "I'm having lamb chops, baked potato, and salad."

Carmen turned, walked into the kitchen, took off her coat, and started preparing the food Lazarus ordered. When everything was prepared, Carmen set it on the dining room table at the place she had set. Going to the door separating the living room from the dining room, she spoke to the back of Lazarus's head, "Your dinner is ready." She then turned and went back into the kitchen where she started cleaning up the items she had used. When she finished cleaning, she sat down at the small table in the corner of the kitchen, folded her hands on the table, and laid her head on her hands. She sat in this position until she heard her name barked by Lazarus in the dining room. "Carmen, I'm finished."

Carmen slowly raised her head, stood, took off all her clothes, and naked, walked into the dining room. She cleared the table of the dishes while Lazarus ran his hands up and down her leg and behind saying, "I love your body, Carmen. We should do this more often."

Carmen, without answering, finished picking up the dishes, pulled herself away, and went back into the kitchen. She finished cleaning the dishes and sat back down, falling into the same position she held before. A half hour passed, then she heard Lazarus with the same bark call out, "Carmen, I'm ready."

Carmen rose, crossed herself, wiped a tear from her eye, and went through the dining room into the living room. Lazarus sat on the sofa naked, facing her, his clothes laying on the floor next to him. "Come closer, Carmen, you do have a beautiful body," he said. He rubbed his hands up and down the sides of her body and between her legs. "Sit down on my lap for a minute," he whispered.

Carmen sat on Lazarus' lap, facing him and straddling his legs. Lazarus started kissing her breasts, still running his hands over her body. After a few minutes he said "Carmen, hang up my clothes."

Carmen slowly got off of Lazarus' lap, bent over and picked up the clothes from the floor, and walked into the bedroom. Lazarus followed and got into the double bed. Carmen finished hanging Lazarus' pants and coat, put the shirt and underwear into a basket sitting in the corner, went to the bed, and lie down spreading her legs apart. Lazarus mounted her, forced her legs further apart, and entered her. Lifting and plunging into her, he started moaning and breathing rapidly, and with one long moan stopped moving. In a few minutes, and what seemed like hours to Carmen, he rolled off her. Carmen slowly sat up, slid her feet off the bed, stood up, went to the basket of dirty clothes, picked them up, and left the room. She walked back into the kitchen, dropping the clothes off on top of the washing machine in the laundry room, a small alcove off of the kitchen. Carmen dressed, put her hair into place with her hands, and left the apartment. It was eight thirty.

Carmen arrived home in twenty minutes. She pulled her 1960 VW Beetle up to the garage door, got out, locked the car, wiped her eyes, and forced a smile onto her face as she entered the house. The four year old boy and six year old girl both yelled, "Mama!" and ran to her, hugging her as she stood by the door. The old lady, sitting in the chair next to the door, was crying. Carmen looked at the old lady, still hugging the children, and said, "Mama, stop that crying right now. What has to be, has to be."

"Why?" the old woman asked in a shaky voice. "I'll go back, I'll go back. Why do you sacrifice yourself for me?"

Carmen, in a much softer voice said, "Mama, if he turns us in to immigration, you will have to go back. Your son, my brother, will have to go back. I can't afford to stay here without his help, or, your help. If we go back, your son will probably end up working in the poppy fields. Your grandchildren might be made to swallow packages of cocaine to bring here. They might end up addicts and die."

"Oh, Jesus, help us please," and the old lady put her face into her hands and softly sobbed.

Maria, the six year old girl said, "Mama, why is Grandma crying?"

"Don't worry, Baby," Carmen said, patting the girl's head. "Old people always cry. It's OK."

Flavia, Carmen's mother looked up, wiping her eyes and said, "Your mama is right. Everything is OK. Come Jorge, let's get ready for a bath."

Carmen said, "Mama, it's George, not Jorge."

"OK," Mama smiled and said, "Come on, George hay," and laughed as she led the boy to the back of the house.

Carmen laughed, bent down and kissed the top of her daughter's head. "Maria," She said, "go get a book and come in the kitchen. I'm going to have the sandwich Grandma made for me, and a glass of milk. I'll read your story while I eat."

"OK, Mama," Maria said and ran to the back of the house.

"Whatever he does to me, this makes it worthwhile. Without him I would be in paradise," she thought.

Carmen went into the kitchen, opened the refrigerator, and took out a dish covered in tin foil and a glass already filled with milk. She set them on the table and sat down. Maria came in carrying three books. Carmen, in mock surprise said, "Maria, three books!"

Maria said, "Mama, please read two books for me."

Carmen laughed, picked Maria up and sat her on her lap, "Well," Carmen drawled out the word, "Since you are so good, I am going to read two books, and because you are so special, I will read the third book, too."

Maria kissed Carmen on the cheek and snuggled against her as Carmen began to read.

CHAPTER 6

Friday turned out to be a busy day for Doris. At nine o'clock Doris and Robin met and discussed the sales of Stylex products, product by product.

"Robin," Doris said, "I've got a project that will take you I don't know how long to do and, I don't know if it will help in any way."

Robin held up her hand and said, "I am here to work. Tell me what you have in mind, and I will get it out as fast as I can. Doing something is a lot better than sitting here knowing what I do will definitely be thrown in the garbage."

They both laughed and Doris said, "Well, if I have to throw it in the garbage, I won't let Robert know, and I will try to hide it from you."

They both laughed again and Doris continued, "Here's my plan. I want a map of the states in which we sell our products. I want you to pin point where the top five sales areas and the lowest five sales areas are, for the top five major products, for the past two years. The financials Deana gave me should have all the figures. I want to see if we can figure out where we can raise awareness in the bad areas, and how we can increase the sales in the good areas. I know we have some national customers, but I want to discuss what would happen if we went national with the advertising of our major products."

"Doris, I will get several wall maps and a thousand colored push pins and start work. This is going to be fun. I am looking forward to seeing Robert's face when you come up with an advertising campaign that goes national."

"Glad you're up for the challenge!" said Doris getting up. "Now, I am going next door to give Brenda her dose of bad news."

Robin laughed, "She will be happy to hear any news you have. This, at least, is doing something that will mean something."

Doris got up, gave the thumbs up sign, and went into Brenda's office. Brenda was sitting back in her chair, a big grin on her face.

"I couldn't help overhearing you and Robin. My desk is clear and I am ready to go. Tell me what you want, and it will be done. And I mean done, post haste".

Doris laughed again, "I'm beginning to have such a good time I don't know if I should get paid for being here. But please, don't tell Stillwell.

As far as I can see, there is little to no advertising targeting the ultimate consumer."

Brenda shot in, "Doris, there is no advertising. That's the problem. But go on. I guess you have already heard that story."

"Yes," Doris said, "You heard Robert already volunteered to edit any advertising campaign I come up with. But, hopefully, Robert and advertising are history."

Brenda said, "Don't underestimate Robert. Bea is his aunt. Although she didn't tell you the other day, Stanley H. and Bea are a definite item and have been for years. Both Everton and Stillwell listen to a lot of what he says."

"Well, hopefully," Doris said, "Stillwell and Everton will give me a chance. If not, then I don't know why I am here."

"Right," Brenda, said, "Now, our main target has been building contractors, remodeling contractors, and big hotel construction companies. I think we could triple our closet systems and kitchen cabinets sales if we went after the women. After all, women account for about eighty percent of the driving force in getting homes remodeled and about one hundred percent when it comes to deciding how to remodel kitchens and closets. Robert only wants to go after the construction industry. He says one sale to a subdivision developer can result in two to six hundred homes. I keep yelling that there are tens of thousands of homes that people are looking to upgrade, not only kitchen and closets, but bathrooms too. If you want, I can show you all my ideas and the ads the agency prepared. All I have to do is drag over the infamous garbage can that Robert keeps putting my stuff in."

"Oh, Brenda, that would be great," Doris said, "Drag over the garbage and let's see if we can get it into the daily papers."

They both laughed, Brenda opened the file drawer behind her and took out three thick folders, laying them on the table at the side of her office. Both she and Doris pulled their chairs to the table, Brenda opened the first file and they spent the next three hours going over advertising copy, making changes to some, putting some back into the proverbial garbage can, and planning the future ad campaign for Stylex.

As they were finishing up, Robert Cleary's voice came from behind them, dripping with sarcasm. "I just wanted to tell you how well your new advertising campaign is doing. Clarence Lucci just called to let me know that, in spite of you, he just sold 437 kitchen and bathroom units with one sales call. And he didn't sell it to some old lady that wants to remodel her kitchen. So how's that for your advertising?"

Doris had turned her chair on hearing Robert's voice. When he finished, she started using a very pleasant, but she thought hopefully, as sarcastic a tone as his. "Robert, come in please. And thank you for knocking. It's nice to see you respecting my privacy. After all, I may have been adjusting my hose, or who knows what else."

Robert opened his mouth to speak but Doris continued with a very loud, "*AND*," she continued, "We are all so proud that Clarence sold, what was it, 227 units."

"437 units." Robert shot in.

"Oh, yes," Doris continued, "407 units, or whatever. I am looking forward to the day when you come running in, all bubbly, and say, Doris, darling, Clarence sold four thousand units today."

Robert looked at Doris and said, "Darling! That'll be the day." He turned and walked out, Doris calling after him. "Thank you, dear."

When the door closed behind Robert, they both started laughing. Robin came in, laughing also and said, "We had better take you to your car when you leave because I think Robert may be waiting to mug you.

"He's starting to aggravate me to the point of distraction. If he keeps up with this I may have to mug him. But, if I let him know he is getting to me, he will just ratchet his sarcasm up a few more levels. What I am trying to do is aggravate him more than he is aggravating me."

34

"Well," Robin said, "I think you are well on your way. When he left, he was definitely not smiling."

"OK," Doris said to Brenda, "how long will it take you to prepare a presentation with the ad agency? When you're ready let me know, and I will call a meeting asking Stillwell and Everton to attend. I will also ask Dietmer Wertzer if he can handle the increased production our new demand will require. And, I will ask the garbage man to attend. I don't want him to think I am leaving him out of the loop. Although, that may not be such a bad idea."

The three girls laughed and Brenda said, "You better be careful. If you make a mistake and call him Garbage Man, he really will hate you forever. But, you asked how long? The presentation is ninety five percent done. I would say I can have a presentation on your desk by Tuesday afternoon. There is a problem though; the agency is going to bill us for another day even though they already billed us for the work. They really are reluctant to come over after dealing with Robert all this time."

"The charge is a reasonable thing taking into account their past dealings with Robert." Doris answered. "Just tell them that there is a new sheriff in town cleaning up the garbage, and we want to be ready for a meeting this coming Friday, say one o'clock. I will confirm the meeting time with you on Monday morning. Now, on Tuesday I will go over your presentation and do my best to pick it to pieces. When I get done with it, you'll think Robert is an angel. So get ready to defend any and everything you give me. Now, go do your dirty work. On Wednesday, when I have finished tearing apart your presentation, we will meet, yell, and scream at each other until we are satisfied with what we want accomplished. Then, you will have Wednesday afternoon and Thursday to prepare for Friday. Meanwhile, Robin and I will spend Monday working out a strategy on what markets to place the ads in. And remember one very important thing, we are presenting what we are going to do. We are not asking permission! Stillwell and Everton said I could have a free hand for at least nine months. Then, I am either right, or out. So come up with some really good ideas."

Brenda smiled, satisfied. "I really am going to love working with you. I believe one hundred percent in what I am saying. If I am wrong you can fire me right before they fire you."

"Oh, girls, I'm sorry." Doris said, "It's five thirty, I have kept you overtime and I also have to get home to my kids. Let's call it a day and we will start over on Monday."

Brenda and Robin said good night as Doris headed out the door. Her car stood alone in the parking lot. There was a truck at the far end of the lot, but she couldn't see if anyone was inside. Not paying too much attention to the lone truck, she unlocked her car and headed for home.

CHAPTER 7

At precisely six o'clock, Woo knocked on the door at 1524 and waited. The door opened; Lazarus stepped back and Woo entered. As Lazarus turned and headed into the living room he said, "Make yourself a drink and let's talk about what we are going to do."

Woo turned and walked into the kitchen, took a glass out of the cabinet, took two ice cubes from the refrigerator, poured scotch from the bottle on the counter into the glass, added water, and walked into the living room. Lazarus was sitting in the middle of the couch, his drink on the coffee table in front of him. Woo sat down in one of the two straight back chairs on the other side of the coffee table, put his drink down, and started, "I think we should..." and stopped as Lazarus started waving his hand.

"Listen, Woo, you've done enough thinking for now. Listen to me for a few minutes. This Bernard tells everyone he is honest. He tells everyone his job as union President is to look out for the workers. And you know what? I think he almost believes it. Now, we are going to tell him that our conversation has to be confidential. He has to believe we are taking him into our trust. I am going to tell the both of you that George is sick. Nobody knows about this yet. Act surprised and a little sad. I'm going to tell Bernard that what we are discussing is only known to us. George wants to increase profits so he can sell the company for big bucks. He is going to protect the workers by giving them large chunks of stock in the company when it is sold."

"That's a great idea," Woo interrupted, "but what if he starts babbling all over the place?"

"We stop him." said Lazarus, "That's your job. As the finance man, you have to convince him that if the word gets out, it will hurt the stock and the workers will suffer. It would all be his fault."

"I think I can do that," said Woo, "but what if he asks about Horworth's involvement? Wait, I know, I'll tell him Horworth wants to keep the stock from the workers so he can have more of it for himself. He's on his way out anyway."

"That's fine," said Lazarus, "but don't tell him he's leaving. Sort of infer that Horworth wants to be President. Let's listen to some music while we wait." And with that he reached behind him and pushed a button. The record fell to the turntable, the needle moved to the edge of the record, and Beethoven's music filled the room.

After about ten minutes of music, with no conversation between Lazarus and Woo, there was a knock at the door. Woo got up, opened the door, and Bill Bernard entered the room. Lazarus went over to Bernard, extended his hand and they shook. "Can I fix you a drink, Bill?" Lazarus asked.

"If you have a beer that would be fine, Mr. Lazarus."

"Please call me Brenton, and do you want a glass or the bottle?"

"Bottle will be fine." Bernard said and turned to Woo. They shook hands as Lazarus went into the kitchen to get a bottle of beer for Bill Bernard. Woo gestured for Bill to follow him into the living room and said, "Why don't you sit on the couch?" Woo then picked up Lazarus' drink and placed it in front of the chair next to where he was sitting and retook his seat. They both sat without speaking while waiting for Lazarus to return.

Bill Bernard sat down on the couch just where Lazarus was sitting moments before and leaned back. Lazarus walked back into the room with a beer and a glass filled with ice and liquid. When he saw Bill on the couch his step faltered, his eyes narrowed, just for a second, and then he continued into the room. He placed the bottle of beer on the table in front of Bill, and sat in the chair next to Woo. Lazarus picked up his drink and held it out. Woo and Bernard held their drinks out in a toast, all taking a sip of their drink.

Lazarus started, "To Stylex. Now, Bill, I want to thank you for taking the time to come here. What I am about to discuss is very sensitive. If this information became public, it could hurt the company. I am counting on your discretion in this matter."

"Mr. Lazarus, Brenton, I want you to know I love this company and would never do anything to hurt it. But, you do realize, that being President of the company union, I have a responsibility to my fellow workers?"

38

Lazarus smiled, "Bill, I know your reputation. The reason I asked you here was just because of your reputation. I know you want what's good for the workers, and for the company."

Lazarus leaned forward and started on the story he'd previously discussed with Woo, about George Stillwell being sick, and that he wanted to build up the company so he could sell it a good price. He told him that he intended to give stock to the workers so they would benefit and wouldn't be left out in the cold. He continued about George and his family being well off and not needing any company money and his strong commitment to protecting the workers.

At this point Lazarus leaned closer to Bill, saying, "One of the ways George wants to build up the company is to move the manufacturing overseas." Lazarus continued, "You know they hired a new lady to punch up sales. We'll probably get more salesmen. As sales start to grow our current plant won't be able to handle the increase in production needed to fill those orders. That is why we will have to set up a plant in China or India to reduce costs and increase profits. When George sees the quality of the work and how cost effective these foreign plants are, he will realize that the best thing for the company, and I must impress upon you the best thing for the workers, is to move the whole operation overseas. When the factory workers hear about a new facility overseas, they will start getting nervous about losing their jobs and start asking you to make demands of George. Now, you know George has always looked out for the people that work for him. If the factory workers want to strike or something, it could hurt the value of the company. In turn, the stock that George will give them will be worth a lot less. If the workers do anything like that, you know George will really be disappointed in them, considering how well he has treated them."

Woo then started his story, "Horworth is trying to talk George into giving management a lot more of the stock. He wants him to stop worrying about the floor workers. Horworth thinks Everton will leave when George does, and he wants to be President, himself."

"Now, Bill," Lazarus continued, cutting Woo off, "we know we are giving you a big job. You have to convince them that an overseas plant is in their best interests without telling them the whole plan. We feel your reputation for honesty, and your knowing the entire picture, makes you the only man that can carry this off. What do you say?"

Bernard put down the beer bottle, leaned back in his chair and closed his eyes. He opened his eyes, leaned forward, and said, "Brenton, you sure have laid a lot on me. I've got to tell you, some of the guys have been mumbling that our jobs are too good to be true, and that one day we are going to be sold out for cheap labor overseas. I know George has treated us better than any other outfit we know of. Every one of us has friends asking if there are any openings over here. I appreciate your taking me into your confidence. I will tell you right now; I will try my best to protect my guys and the company. "

"I knew we could count on you, Bill," Lazarus said, "If you ever have any questions, or learn of anything that will help us, just get in touch with Woo here. I think you coming to see me at the plant will get people talking. Oh, and there is something else. When we start setting up overseas, we will need a team, say about five people, to oversee production, you know, to make sure we get quality stuff. We will need someone to lead this team. It would mean a five year contract with a starting salary of seventy five thousand dollars and a thirty thousand dollar a year living allowance. I would like you to consider this job for yourself. If, however, you would be unable to go, we would understand, but, would ask you to give us the names of three people and a list of five others that you think might qualify to fill out the team."

"That sounds like a fantastic job," Bill said as he started to pick up the beer bottle, putting it down because of his hand trembling. "Would the person that went overseas be able to bring a wife?" he added.

Lazarus smiled, "Bill, if the person you recommend has a wife, I am sure she can be hired as his assistant at, say, forty thousand a year. Of course, there would be no living allowance for her."

Bill took a deep breath, looked from Lazarus to Woo and back again. He took another deep breath and started, "As I said, you really laid a lot on me tonight. I have been here five years and somehow, I'm not sure how, I ended up as President of our union. I don't know why we have a union. We are treated so much better than any other plant around; it's hard to believe. As I said, all the guys tell me they have dozens of friends that would love to come to work here. No one I know would do anything to hurt this company. They know George won't screw them. You tell me when and I will do my damnedest to keep everyone in line.

Oh," Bill continued, "and I think I can put together a group for you that could honcho those overseas workers into a streamlined factory."

"That's great, "said Lazarus, "thanks for coming over." Lazarus stood, extending his hand, and continued, "I am sure I can depend on your discretion in this matter."

Bill stood, shook Lazarus' hand, turned to Woo, shook his hand and said, "I appreciate you both taking me into your confidence. I won't let you down."

The three men walked to the door. Lazarus opened the door and said, "Thank you, Bill. Remember, if you have any questions or concerns, please call Woo."

Bill walked out and Lazarus closed the door.

Woo opened his mouth to speak but, Lazarus shook his head quickly back and forth, and Woo closed his mouth without speaking.

They stood by the door until they heard the elevator door open and then close. Lazarus walked back to the living room, retook his seat on the couch, and smiled. "Well, Woo, I think we have a partner; yes definitely, a partner. The only thing left on the agenda is to handle that useless skirt, Doris Wilcox. I've already got things rolling on that front, though."

"I should've known you'd have everything handled. This sounds fantastic. Hell," Woo said, "I would like to take that job overseas. And I'll even take my wife along."

Lazarus shook his head, "Woo, you idiot, there is no job overseas. When this is done we just hire a manufacturer overseas to do the work. As long as the quality is passable it will be fine. Remember, when the company is sold, our stock will make us millionaires."

"I knew that." Woo said with a half-smile on his face. He picked up his glass, emptied it, put it down on the table, turned, and walked out of the apartment without saying another word.

CHAPTER 8

In the Marketing Department, Doris got up from her desk, shook her head, picked up her pocketbook, and walked out into the outer office. "Alice, I am going home. I cannot cram another bit of information into my head today." She then called out, "Nice job, Brenda. Robin, will you be ready for me tomorrow morning?"

Robin yelled back, "Doris, I am ready to fight you tooth and nail. And I'll bring the coffee."

Doris smiled, waved to Alice and left the office. She opened the door to the parking lot and found Forman talking to one of the shop workers. He looked up and nodded to Doris.

Doris nodded and said, "Have a nice night, Albert."

The other man took a step backwards and looked back and forth between Forman and Doris. He looked like he was ready to run from the scene.

"Thanks, Doris," Forman said and turned back to continue his conversation.

When Doris got into her car she banged the steering wheel with her hand. "Damn." She said. "I am supposed to bring an apple pie for the dinner with the girls at Anna's house." She put the car in gear, stopped at the first bakery she came to, and headed home.

As soon as she opened the door, the girls were at her side, all dressed and ready to go. "We're all ready to go. We've been ready for an hour." Margaret said.

They all left the house at the same time. Doris strapped the two girls in the back seat, one in a booster seat, the other strapped in with the shoulder strap behind her head, and then got into the car. Margaret got into her own car, waved, and they both left.

Following Margaret's directions, Doris pulled into the driveway of Anna Maxwell's house. As she was getting out of the car, the back door flew open and Mary Wilcox bolted out of the car, running full tilt for the front door of Aunt Anna's house. Susan was screaming for

Doris to unbuckle her. By the time Susan was unbuckled and Doris picked up the pie from the front seat, the front door was open and Anna's nieces, Mary and Joan, were jumping up and down while Anna stood smiling at the scene. Doris approached, shifting the pie into her left hand, extending her right hand.

The ladies shook hands and Doris said, "Hello, Aunt Anna, I'm Doris Wilcox."

Anna laughed, "You don't have to call me Aunt. Just call me Anna. And I won't call you Mama."

Doris smiled, "That's fair. And here is dessert. That's if they eat all their supper."

"Oh, I think they will," Anna said, "I have salad, spaghetti and meatballs, garlic bread, and cherry Crystal Light for drink. And for you and me, I have a very nice red wine that really goes well. We'll let them play for a little while after supper before we have the apple pie and a glass of milk. How does that sound?

"I'm ready," Doris said, "what can I do to help? By the way, please call me DD, all my friends do."

Anna said, "Alright, DD, here are silverware and dishes including plastic for the little girls." Doris carried the tableware out and set the table with six settings, the two plastic plates and cups in front of the booster seats, the regular plates at the remaining four seats. Anna came out with a steaming bowl of spaghetti and meatballs, placed it on the table and called to the girls, "Girls, time to wash your hands and get ready for dinner."

Doris asked, "Anybody need to go potty first?"

Joan answered yes and Susan chimed in with a, "me too."

Doris said, "Show me where the bathroom is."

Joan took her hand, Susan quickly grabbed the other hand and Doris was led away.

The older girls finished washing their hands, leaving Doris with the younger two girls, and quickly ran back to the dining room. The girls sat at the table with a lot of talking and laughing, waiting for dinner to be served. Anna handed Doris a tray with a bowl of salad, a separate bowl of finely cut tomatoes, cucumbers, and celery. Anna then picked up a steaming bowl of spaghetti covered with sauce, and a bowl of meatballs that were also covered with sauce.

"Now," Anna said, "My girls will have one piece of lettuce and two spoons of the tomato, cucumber, celery mixture."

Doris stopped and looked at Anna. "You know, Anna," she said, "that's really scary. My girls eat salad the same way."

Anna smiled and said, "Well, I guess it's true. They all do have the same teacher."

Doris served helpings of the tomato, cucumber, celery mixture onto four plates, putting them in front of Anna, who then added a meatball and a fork full of spaghetti. Then they started cutting up the meatballs into small bite size pieces and cutting the spaghetti into short strips. The plates were put in front of the girls, napkins tucked into their shirts, and the girls started eating. Anna and Doris helped themselves to the food and sat slowly eating, watching the girls with love oozing out of their eyes.

After dinner, while the girls quietly played, Anna whispered to Doris, "They get along better than I did growing up with my sister. I always fought with her."

"Where is your sister?" Doris asked.

"Oh," Anna answered, "She and her husband are out west. They run the family farm my folks had. I guess you would call it a, farm ranch. Half the acreage is wheat, and the other half is used to raise cattle. We were almost self-sufficient, raising enough wheat to feed the herd of cattle my folks had. I have one sister and one brother. When my brother's wife died I came here to take care of his kids so he could do his salesman job. He really enjoys the selling. He works for the same company you do. He is always going out of town or working odd hours, so I volunteered to be the nanny. I love it."

"I know what you mean," Doris answered. "I just can't wait to get home each day to see what they have learned. They just seem to soak up information at an amazing rate. If it continues until they are fifteen they will be ten times as smart as Einstein. Since I just started at Stylex, I don't know many of the salesman yet."

Anna, with a big smile on her face said, "The girls are amazing. I'm so thrilled at how fast they've taken to each other."

Doris turned to look at the four girls playing at the other end of the room. The two Marys were busy dressing the younger girls in play clothes, each dressing the other's sister. Each one was showing their model how to hold their hands on their hips, and how to strut back and forth for the fashion show they were preparing.

"It is wonderful how they seem to get along so well," Anna said, "and thank goodness, without the sibling rivalry that is a part of growing up. My sister and I laugh about it now that we have our separate lives. Do you have any siblings, DD?"

"No, I am an only child. My mother had three miscarriages before I was born. The doctors told her it would be dangerous for her to try again. They live out in California in a retirement village. I used to get out there every couple of months while my husband was alive. Now I try to get out there at least three times a year, and sometimes more, if I can get time off from the job."

"Oh, I'm so sorry," said Anna. "My brother's wife got hit with cancer. It was less than five months before she was gone. Was your husband sick?"

"No," Doris answered, "my husband was a colonel in the Air Force. He had sixty combat missions without a scratch. Then he took a kid, actually a young cadet, on a training flight. I was told the young man rolled the plane over and dived. When it came time for him to pull out, he instinctively pulled the stick forward and drove the plane into the ground. Sixty combat missions with nothing and a stupid mistake ended it all. Benefits are great, but I just couldn't sit home. I was getting more and more depressed. This way, I get out and involved, interacting, and fighting with people. I've always had fun working. And this job is going to be great. And I tell you, I am interacting, and I really am going to have to fight some Neanderthal that still thinks a woman's place is in the home."

Anna laughed, "There are a million of them out there. You have to change them or kill them. I think sometimes it is just easier to kill them."

Anna's niece, Mary, came over to the ladies and said, "OK, Aunt Anna and Mama, you have to sit down to watch our show. We can clean up the supper dishes after our show, then have dessert!"

"I think you have to say Mrs. Wilcox when you talk to Mary's mother. It's the proper way to address an adult."

"Oh, it's OK, Aunt Anna," Mary answered. "Mary said she calls you Aunt and I can call her mother, Mama. That way we can really be like big sisters to Joan and Susan"

Doris shrugged, "I guess you just can't argue with that logic. OK to you Mary. You can call me Mama. Aunt Anna and Mama will sit down and watch your show."

The ladies sat as the older girls instructed the younger two on how to walk back and forth in front of their audience. Then the top layer of clothes was removed revealing another layer of clothing for the next walk. The girls had dressed their sisters in five layers of clothes and had them walk back and forth. Anna and Doris were clapping, and laughing, for each walk the girls made. At the end, the girls lined up for hugs and went back to see what other games they could play.

Doris and Anna started clearing the table. Doris rinsed the dishes and put them in the dishwasher while Anna put away the leftovers. When they were done they went back to the living room and Doris said, "OK, girls, it's time to go."

With that announcement came a lot of begging and pleading for a little while longer.

"Come on now, girls," Doris said, "we have a long ride home, you have to take a bath and then it will be past your bedtime."

Anna added, "Yes, girls, go home and get a good night's sleep. Tomorrow, you can tell all your friends at school what a great party you had. I am sure they will want to hear everything."

They all agreed that was a good idea. All the girls hugged. Doris thanked Anna for a great time and, of course, Anna thanked Doris for bringing her girls over. As they got to the door Anna said, "DD, how about next Tuesday? The girls are so good together, I think we should make this a weekly dinner party. And hopefully next time

46

you can meet my brother. He would love seeing the girls play together."

Doris said, "I would love to. Can I bring anything other than dessert?"

"You just bring dessert and don't worry about anything else." Anna answered.

***

It was eleven thirty when Robert Cleary got home. He stopped in the kitchen, took a bottle of beer from the refrigerator, turned to the counter for a bottle opener, and found a note from Anna that read, "Kids had a great time at their play date. See you in the morning."

CHAPTER 9

Bill Bernard arrived at his apartment, unlocked the door, and walked in to a small foyer. From the living room came a voice, "Well, what did Woo and the other idiot want?"

Bill walked into the living room to see Betty English, his girlfriend curled up on the couch in a bright red pair of pajamas. "I can't discuss it with anyone," he said.

"What?" came the reply, as Betty uncurled from the couch and approached Bill, her brow furrowed. "Listen to me, Mr. Secret Agent. If you don't want a miserable time here you better open up. And besides, you're going to tell me before the night is out anyway. You know you can't keep a secret for long. So let's cut the crap and tell me what the hell is so secret, and what is going on?"

"Well, damn," Bill said, "Don't have an attack. Sit down and I will tell you the whole story." Betty sat back down and Bill sat at the other end of the couch facing her. "First of all, this President of the union shit is about to drive me crazy. I don't know what interests of the men, oh, and of the women," Bill quickly added, "I am supposed to protect."

Betty smiled and said, "I'll tell you later, just go on with your story. And you are right. We need a union like shit needs a smell."

"Betty, you are so colorful and refined I can hardly stand it." Bill laughed and continued, "Well, this very hush-hush secret meeting was to tell me we are going to open a plant overseas, and that this factory will be shut down."

Betty opened her mouth to speak, but Bill held up his hand "Let me tell you the whole story, will you? Now, they are telling me this story, so listen. They said," Bill paused, "Actually I don't know why Woo was there. He seemed to be afraid of Lazarus, I mean really afraid. Anyway, Lazarus is telling me that George is sick, and he is going to make the company very profitable by moving production overseas. Then George is going to give all his stock to us – the workers,

I mean. After that, he is planning to sell the company and all the workers will be millionaires."

"What a crock of shit," Betty blurted out. "George is not sick. What's wrong with George? There isn't even a rumor of George being sick."

Bill pointed a finger at Betty, shook his head back and forth and said, "Betty, will you please let me get my story out? What he wants me to do is, when the rumor gets out that we are going to shut down the plant here in the states and move over to China or India, or wherever, tell the men, and the women, that they should be happy. They say, I should tell them to keep working hard, and they will be millionaires. They told me that Joe Everton and Stanley Horworth are against the move because they want George to give them all the stock."

Betty leaned forward, and opened her mouth to speak. Bill held up his finger again, and Betty closed her mouth and leaned back.

Bill continued, "Now to keep me happy, I will be going to China, or wherever, and heading up a management team, at double my salary with a living allowance and a big bonus. I can bring my wife along and she will also have a job with big bucks."

Betty jumped up and started yelling, "Wife! What wife? You don't have a wife. What the hell are you talking about? You're not married, you son of a bitch. What the hell is going on?"

Bill looked up at her, smiling and said, "You! I was talking about you. I was talking about taking you, my wife, along with me. Hello! You! Wife!" Betty looked at him for several seconds then jumped into his lap and furiously started kissing his face. Then she stopped, got off his lap and looked at him, put her hands on her hips and started, "What if I don't want to go to China, or wherever?" Then she sat down and looked at him and continued, "And, what if I don't want to marry you? You haven't even asked me yet."

Bill slid off the couch onto one knee in front of Betty, took her hand and looked up at her. He said, "Betty English, will you become my wife?"

Betty looked at him, tears started running down her cheeks, "Yes, oh, yes I will." And she pulled Bill up onto the couch and starting kissing him again. After a lot of kissing she said, "When are we going to get married? When are we moving to China?"

Bill answered, "Whenever you want. And, we are not moving to China."

Betty looked at him and patting his cheek said, "But, I thought they made you a fantastic offer. With all that money, after five years, we would be rich."

Bill sighed, "They had me going for a while. Everything they said made sense, except about all the workers becoming millionaires. They had me sold; hook, line and sinker. Then they threw in this shit about needing someone to tell the Chinese how to run a factory, and how they were going to pay me over a hundred grand a year to do nothing for five years. Don't you see, Betty? It was a bribe. When I left, I told them they could count on me. I told them I loved the company and would look out for the men, and I wouldn't tell a soul. Except for you, of course," Bill smiled gave Betty a long tender kiss.

When he lifted his head, Betty said, "Bill, I love you so much."

"I love you so much, too," Bill answered and leaned back next to Betty. "Can you believe all that shit?" Bill sighed, "I don't know what to do now. I was thinking of going to Everton or Horworth, but what if I am wrong and they are telling the truth. I will really be in deep shit."

Betty laughed, "There sure is a lot of shit going around here tonight. What about you going to the top? Stillwell ought to know if he is sick or not and if he is going to get everyone fired. Anyway, I can't believe George would sell us down the river. Everyone is getting paid double here compared with other companies."

"Yeah," Bill said, "but as soon as I head to the front office the whole world is going to know. I am going to have to think about this for a while and then make a decision."

"Enough of this already," Betty said, "Let's talk about something important."

"Important?" Bill, looking surprised, said, "What, this isn't important?"

"Not really," Betty smiled. "What is important is, when are we going to get married? I have to call my folks, get a gown, hire a hall, check out some bands, and get a caterer. We need to make a list of wedding guests. Oh my God, there is so much to do."

"I've got a great idea." Bill said, looking a little panicky, "Why don't we elope?"

"Oh, Bill, darling, I love you, I love you," Betty said. "Just be quiet and don't interrupt my dream."

"I think I have created a monster," Bill laid back on the couch, a satisfied grin on his face.

CHAPTER 10

Joe Everton called, "Grace, come in here please." Grace walked into Everton's office with pad and pencil, ready to take dictation. "No dictation," he said, "just set up a meeting with Robert and Ivan for some time this afternoon. I want to discuss an idea George and I have been talking about."

"What idea is that, Dad?" Grace asked.

"Even though everyone here knows you are my daughter, I would appreciate you not calling me Dad. Just call me Joe," he admonished her.

"Dad, eh, Joe, I told you, it is so hard for me to call my father by his first name." Grace replied. "And when I call you Mr. Everton everyone laughs. Oh, alright, Joe, what idea are you and George talking about?"

"I will discuss it with you when the time is right. Now would you set up that meeting with them for this afternoon?"

Grace turned, gave a roll of her head and walked out. She called Robert and confirmed a two o'clock time and then called Ivan Lucci, the director of the New Product division, and got his approval of the two o'clock meeting time.

At the same time, but on a different floor, Doris entered her office carrying four cups of coffee in one of those cardboard cup holders, put a cup on Alice's desk, Brenda's desk, and on the way into her office said, "Today is a real work day. Alice, please help Brenda with whatever she needs. Robin, bring all your stuff into my office. I have our coffees."

Robin picked a stack of papers up off her desk and entered Doris's office right behind her saying, "Looks like you are raring to go."

Doris answered, "I had a great weekend with my kids. I played with them, napped with them, and went to bed the same time they did. I haven't had so much sleep in, I don't remember when. Now, I am ready to conquer the world, or at least Stylex. What have you got for me?"

Robin unrolled a black and white, three by four foot, map of the United States, with red, green, and blue dots clustered around Kentucky, Tennessee, Ohio, Indiana, Illinois, and a few in Kansas and Iowa. Then she started, "When the company started, their goal was to have their products put into new homes. Stillwell had a bunch of builders he knew, and their business got him started. But, he didn't have enough business with those, so he targeted builders in other areas. He hired salesmen with the goal of hitting the major builders outside the immediate area. It was touch and go for a while, then Arthur Wertzer, that's Dietmar's brother, connected with four builders in upper Ohio. Another salesman, his name was Bert Moses, came in with some great orders from Indiana."

Doris interrupted, "What do you mean, his name was Bert Moses? What happened to him?"

Robin answered, "He was killed in a car crash while he was on the road about four years ago. That's when Robert came in. Stillwell is still paying Moses' salary to his family. He had three kids. Stillwell is paying for college for two of the kids and will pay for the other one when he starts next year. Arthur Wertzer had a heart attack and died, and his family got his salary until his wife remarried. She had to tell Stillwell to stop sending the salary checks. She told him she married a man with a lot of money. Doris, that man is so generous it's unbelievable. He's only fired one man that I know of and that was for stealing. And he gave him a month's salary. Anyway, when Robert came in he just continued going in the same direction. As far as I know, they never tried getting our stuff into furniture stores or home improvement centers.

Now these colored dots represent completed orders for the last four years. That's the years Robert had me keeping records. The red dots are where the builders used both bathroom and kitchen packages. The green dots are those builders that only used our kitchen packages, and the blue dots are those who used our bathroom packages. He never did separate out those who did or did not use our closet packages."

"OK," Doris said, "we've got a good presence in Kentucky, Tennessee, Ohio, Indiana and Illinois so I think we should hit the individual home owners in those markets. A lot of those looking to refurbish may have friends that already have our equipment in their homes. Now what about our suppliers? Can we count on them? You know, like, we sell quality products to Stylex, and Stylex makes quality products to sell to you, or something like that."

Robin opened a file and set three pages in front of Doris and started to explain them. "These are our thirty largest suppliers with addresses, phone numbers, and contacts. There are four listed that I cannot find any information on. But I think twenty six will give us enough to work with, don't you think?"

"No information on four of our largest suppliers does seem odd." Doris said, then shrugged her shoulders and continued, "We'll worry about that later. Let's color in some dots where these are located and see how it ties in with our sales areas."

Doris started reading out addresses and Robin started putting black dots on the map. When they were finished, Doris looked at the map nodding her head.

"Well," she said, "It looks like twenty two of our suppliers are in the areas of our greatest sales and the other six will help us open up new territory. We'll have to ask Deana about the other four. OK, leave this stuff with me and let me chew on it for a while. You know what else you can do for me? You can make a list of a dozen or so home improvement centers in our target areas with the names of the buyers. It may be a good idea to invite them to see our setup, all expenses paid of course. That way, Robert can do his selling job. I just hope he doesn't sabotage our efforts."

"I don't think he will," Robin said, "He may be a pain in the ass and all that, but I don't think he will knowingly do anything to hurt the company."

"We'll see," Doris continued, "And if they handle our product, they will have to get a group of carpenters or handy men to install our kitchen and bathroom packages. Our closet systems will probably be done by homeowners themselves in many cases. It's not that complicated. Maybe we'll ask the buyers to bring one or two of their favorite installers with them when they come for their all expense vacation."

"I'm on it." Robin said. "Do you want me to check with Deana on the other four?"

"No," Doris answered, "It's not that important. I'll ask her the next time I see her."

Robin departed and Doris sat back looking at the map and at the other papers that Robin left behind. She started making notes.

At two o'clock both Robert and Ivan entered Joe's outer office, both greeted Grace. Robert said, "What's going on?"

Grace looked at Robert and said, "Why ask me?" Sometimes he treats me like some kind of spy. Just a minute, I'll see if he's ready." Grace opened the door to Joe Everton's office and said, "They're here."

Everton looked up, smiled "Thanks, Darling, bring them in."

"You better watch out," Grace said, "I can sue for sexual harassment."

"OK, Peanut," Everton laughed, "But send them in anyway."

Grace backed away from the open door laughing, nodded her head toward the door, and stood by the door as they entered. She then followed them in to room.

"Take a seat, guys" he said, and looked over to where Grace was standing.

"Yes, Ms. Donald," Everton said in a somber voice, "Is there something you need?"

"I'm ready to take notes for this meeting, and I just wanted to know if anyone wanted coffee before we start," Grace said. She stood there with a straight face but had a twinkle in her eyes that was hard to hide.

Before either Robert or Ivan had a chance to speak, Everton laughed and said, "Nobody wants coffee, or anything else, and I will dictate the notes of this meeting some other time. Please close the door on your way out, Ms. Donald. Thank you."

"Huh," Grace said," she turned, walked out, and closed the door a little harder than was required.

Everton laughed, "Boy, it is tough having a daughter working for you. I'm in for a rough time until she finds out what's going on here."

Robert laughed "Well, Ivan and I want to know what's going on too. I've heard rumors the company is going to shut down, and then I heard we were being sold. Next, I heard we're moving overseas, which may not be a bad idea, except it's going to displace a lot of people."

"It is so amazing to me," Joe said shaking his head. "I think of something, or George and I have dinner together and mention something, and before I can get back to work there are rumors floating around that hit on exactly what I was thinking or what George and I were talking about. I wonder how they do it."

Ivan and Robert were both laughing when Ivan said, "Joe, there are only so many bad things that can happen around here. And what's the use of rumors about good things happening."

They all laughed, and then Joe leaned forward and started. "All right, all the rumors are true."

Both men stiffened, looked at each other and then back at Joe, who smiled and continued, "Well, all except shutting down. Here's the deal. George wants to get out. I want to get out and so does Stanley H... We were talking about moving production overseas, either to China or India, and leaving administration and sales right here. Maybe we'd start a sales force in England. Apartments in England are so small they need our cabinet and shelving systems to better utilize the space they have. Anyway, that leaves Lazarus and Woo to run the company. George, and I too, have a funny feeling about those two running the company. So, then we talked about selling the company. The way George has been giving out bonuses, our bottom line doesn't make us a good candidate for a sale. You know, almost half the production staff started with George and were working for minimum wage when he hardly had money to pay them that."

"He sure made up for that, to those guys, and to the rest of us," Ivan said. "My brother-in-law is Production Chief in a shop over in Tennessee, and he makes about half of what I do. Every time we talk he wants to know if there are any openings here. He says he is ready to move."

Joe smiled, "George says before he leaves here, he will definitely take care of everyone.

He's been talking to an architect who has a brilliant idea. I think it is a scary thing to try and make work, but he wants us to examine it, and afterwards meet with him, and tell him why it won't work. This architect has a small company that has run out of money. This company was being set up to build houses."

"What's so scary about that?" Robert asked. "Building houses isn't scary."

Joe smiled, "They want to build the houses in a factory."

"Joe," Ivan said, "They have been building houses in factories for a long time. They call them mobile homes. What are we talking about?"

"Listen to me, will you," Joe said, "I am talking about building, what I guess could be called, stick built houses, except there won't be any sticks. They're talking about putting down a slab with plumbing roughed out; setting in an outline of the house's exterior and interior walls; bolting this outline down to the slab; installing flooring to the outline; and then trucking in wall segments with electricity already embedded in these wall segments. There will be windows in the exterior walls and doorjambs set into the interior walls. A crew will bolt these segments together, set the roof trusses, lay the roof, and be done. They figure about two or three days to complete a house after the slab is done. These wall segments are of some kind of polymer, light and strong. The engineers estimate they will easily withstand one hundred forty mile an hour winds without falling down. Although, the roof will probably blow off. For now, it will have a standard roof, but they are working on a single unit roof that will have shingles as an integral part of the roof."

Both Ivan and Robert sat looking at Joe without speaking, not knowing if he was funning with them or if he was serious.

"OK, let me continue," Joe said. "The factory is almost ready. There are seventy specialty trucks that can carry three quarters of a house. George has about seven thousand acres of land, all spread out over the surrounding states, that he wants to use to develop small, three or four hundred home communities, on half-acre plots. He figures he can put these things on the market for about thirty to thirty five dollars a foot including land."

"That's about twenty dollars a foot less than the market." Robert finally said. "If it's too cheap, people will think there is something wrong with it. And the polymer, can you hammer a nail into it? How thick are the walls? What about sound? Will you be able to hear everything from room to room? Do they have various ceiling heights? How many models will they be able to show? What about a two story model?" Robert kept asking these questions without waiting for an answer.

"Whoa, whoa," Joe laughed, "That's about a dozen questions. I want you guys to take a trip with me. Ivan, Robert, you two live close to each other. One of you can pick up the other, and the two of you pick me up at my house at about five. We should be back Tuesday night sometime. Don't have your families wait on you for dinner. We will probably eat something on the road. And do me a big favor. Please let's not get any rumors started for a while. I really would appreciate your not telling your wife, or family, or even your dog about this. Let's see if we can hold the rumors for at least a couple of weeks."

Both men rose and Robert said, "I won't even tell my kids."

They all laughed and the two men left the office. As soon as Ivan shut Joe's door, Grace said, "OK, what's the big deal?"

Robert leaned over and whispered, "Were not supposed to say anything but since you're family," he leaned closer and said, "Your father is planning to start a circus and he wants us to be clowns."

Grace leaned back and looked at the two men. "Well I guess he picked the two best men for the job." They all started laughing and the two men walked out of the office.

Robert got to his office and Bea said, "You and Ivan were in talking to Joe such a long time. Are you solving the woes of the world?"

"Oh, nothing important." Robert smiled at her, "I am going home now. Cancel whatever I have for tomorrow. I'll be back Wednesday morning."

"What about the sales meeting you have for tomorrow morning?" Bea asked.

"Oh," Robert paused, "Charlie and Clarence can take care of that. Tell them I had a family emergency, and I had to go out of town. Give the notes on my desk to Charlie and tell him to pump the guys up a little. OK, I got to go."

Robert turned to leave but Bea stopped him. "Wait a minute. You and Ivan meet with Joe, and you have a family emergency, and, you're going out of town?"

"I didn't want to have to tell you," Robert said, "But I am running away to get married."

"Thank, God." Bea said, "My condolences to the poor thing you're eloping with. So you're not going to tell me what is going on. You know, I'll find out quick enough."

"Listen, Bea," Robert said, "Nothing is going on. I just can't say where we are going."

"We, Robert," Bea said, "Who is we?"

"Jesus, Bea, do you work for the CIA or something? Nothing else? I am out of here."

Robert left, leaving Bea laughing as she bent over the files continuing to make notes.

Meanwhile, back in Everton's office, Grace answered the phone on the second ring, "Mr. Everton's office, Grace speaking."

"Let me talk to Joe," Lazarus barked, "This is Mr. Lazarus."

"Yes, I know, Brenton," Grace answered, in a voice she hoped showed some degree of contempt. Emphasizing the word mister, she responded, "*Mr.* Everton is on the other line, can I have him call you back?"

"Tell him I want to see him for a half hour; I want to know a good time." Brenton said, and hung up the phone.

Grace looked at the phone, slowly shook her head and hung up the receiver. When she saw the light go out on the phone indicating Everton had hung up the phone, she got up, went to his door, opened it and when her father looked up said, "Brenton wants to see you for a half hour this afternoon."

Everton looked at his watch and grunted, "A half hour for Brenton will end up being an hour. Tell him to be here at three thirty, and when you're done with that, bring in your pad. I want you to write a letter."

Grace nodded, closed the door, went to her desk, picked up the phone, and dialed. When the phone was answered, she said, "Mr. Everton said to come up at three thirty." She hung up the phone, not waiting for an answer. Picking up her pad and pencil, she walked back into her father's office and sat in the chair in front of his desk.

Everton leaned back in his chair and started, "This goes to Mr. Merle Rotah. That's with an H on the end. The address is here," and he handed Grace a letter. "Send this," he continued, "Both George Stillwell and I appreciated meeting with you and your board of directors. While we were impressed with your offer, we are not, at this time, interested in selling Stylex. Mr. Stillwell has several unique ideas. While he feels they would be revolutionary in the business, they could have strong negative consequences to the bottom line. He is reluctant to burden anyone else with this possibility. We will continue to explore other ways that we could unite. Give our best regards to your board, and thank them for meeting with us. Sincerely."

As Grace was leaving the office Everton said, "We're going out to dinner Wednesday night. Do you and Jerry want to join us?"

"I'd love to, Dad," Grace turned and answered, "However, I have a study group Wednesday night and Jerry is studying for a big test coming up on Thursday. What about the end of the week or the weekend?

"OK," Everton replied, "Your mother will call you."

At three thirty Lazarus walked into the office and, ignoring Grace, walked to the closed door of Everton's office, opened it and walked in. Without a greeting or waiting for one he said, "Listen Joe, I didn't mean to blow my stack about the financials that Deana was giving out. I guess I am a little paranoid. Now, if the woman is as good as you all think and starts bringing in a lot of new business what are we going to do to increase out capacity to meet the new demand? A lot of the men are getting on, and you know they don't move as fast as before. I know George is really loyal to these men, so, I was thinking, why not get another plant to handle the overflow? I've been checking around and a lot of the manufacturers I've talked to are letting the Chinese handle their manufacturing. Even with the transportation, we could reduce our costs. Why don't you discuss it with George? It will take a while to set up overseas, and we shouldn't wait for the last minute."

"I'm glad to see you think Doris can accomplish such an increase in our sales. I thought you were against changing our sales focus and hiring her. I will discuss this with George, although, I know he is against sending our manufacturing overseas if it will displace his people. He won't do anything to hurt them."

Lazarus then went into a long description of the benefits of overseas manufacturing, sharing all he had learned about the various areas of China that would be best suited for Stylex. He kept talking, repeating himself frequently, while Everton kept looking at his watch. Finally, Everton held up his hand to stop Lazarus and said, "Brenton, I'm sorry, I promised Joyce I would be home early today, and it is getting past the time she is expecting me. I will talk to George and let you know what he says."

"Oh, sure." Lazarus said, "Keep me posted." He turned and walked out of the office.

CHAPTER 11

Lazarus walked back to the plant assembly floor, to Forman's office. He stuck his head in the door and said, "Hey, Forman, you got the paper work for my inventory control report"

"Sure do." and Forman handed Lazarus a stack of papers. Then Forman said, "Brenton, you better check out two new suppliers we've got. I've got receipts for merchandise from them, but I haven't had a chance to check on the actual delivery of the stuff."

"I'll check on it when I review all these papers. Just keep everything quiet and running as usual."

"Hey, Brenton," Forman answered back, "You're setting up a fund for the guys and that is important. If we all are about to lose our jobs when they move production overseas, we need some protection. A lot of these guys have been here as long as I have. If they lose their jobs, they won't have anything. How will you divide the funds?"

As he was leaving Lazarus said, "I'll find a way. Probably by longevity is the best way." When Lazarus got to his own office he told Elizabeth to hold his calls, went into his office, and spread out the papers Forman gave him on his desk, arranging them by supplier's name. He immediately was able to identify the two new suppliers that Forman asked about. Two invoices for each one. The first one, Dragon Iron Purveyors had one invoice for nine thousand three hundred dollars and the other for eight thousand three hundred dollars. The second new supplier, Tiger Steel Company had one invoice for eight thousand three hundred dollars and the other for nine thousand three hundred dollars. He sat and looked at the invoices for a few minutes. He slowly picked up his phone and dialed the phone number on the first invoice. The recording came back saying, "No such number, please check the listing and dial again." He hung up the phone and then dialed the phone number of the other supplier getting the same recording. He hung up and dialed three numbers. When the Accounting Department phone rang, Carmen answered, "Accounting, Carmen speaking."

Lazarus, in his usual tone to Carmen barked, "I want a list of the checks for the last two months for the companies I gave you and I want it now."

Carmen hung up the phone, turned to her computer screen, and started writing information from the screen onto a pad listing; date, check number, payee, and amount of checks payable to Dragon Iron Purveyors, Master Iron Works, Metal Fabricators, and Tiger Steel Company. She tore off the sheet of paper, folded it, and put it in an envelope. She got up, walked to the door, looked back, and said, "I'll be right back. I have to take this information up to Mr. Lazarus."

"Boy, I sure would like to know why she is so afraid of that son of a bitch." Susan said.

"Yeah," Frances said, "guaranteed it's not love."

Carmen walked into Lazarus' office and said to Elizabeth Cooper, his secretary, "I've got to give this to Mr. Lazarus."

"OK, give it to me and I will take it in to him." Elizabeth said.

"No," Carmen said, holding the envelope closer to her chest, "I have to give it to him myself."

Elizabeth nodded her head toward the closed door and Carmen went to it, opened it, and keeping her eyes down, walked over to the desk where Lazarus sat and put the envelope on his desk. Without saying a word, she turned and walked out, closing the door behind her. She entered the Accounting Department, saw Susan and Frances looking at her, and said, "What's wrong?"

Susan said, "He wants you in his office and right now. He sounded so mad. I thought he was going to come through the phone. You better take off."

Before Susan was finished speaking, Carmen was gone. When she got back upstairs she rushed right past Elizabeth and without knocking, opened the door, walked in, closed the door, and said, "What's wrong, Mr. Lazarus? What did I do wrong?"

Lazarus threw the paper across the desk. The paper slid off the desk and fell to the floor in front of Carmen. She bent down and picked up the papers looking at them.

"Well?" he said.

"I'm sorry, Mr. Lazarus," Carmen stammered. "I don't know what's wrong."

"Are you an idiot?" Lazarus whispered. "I asked for two months of checks. That is a total of four checks. You have listed eight checks. Who the hell are Dragon Iron Purveyors and Tiger Steel Company? Why are they listed? What the hell's going on? Are you crazy?"

"Sir," Carmen said in a hysterical voice, "Mr. Woo said you authorized these two additional companies. He said they were to be handled in the usual manner. He said, you said, it was to be handled in the same manner as these other checks. I gave the checks to Mr. Woo personally, as usual. Please ask Mr. Woo. He will tell you that is what he said."

"Get out," Lazarus hissed. When Carmen didn't move he shouted, "Get out, I said!"

Carmen turned and ran out of the office not stopping long enough to close his door. She ran into the hallway, down to the ladies room, entered a stall, bent over, and threw up. She stood leaning against the door, waiting for her heart to stop pounding. She stood there for five minutes before she felt well enough to move. She then opened the stall door, went to the sink, rinsed out her mouth, washed and dried her face, and left the bathroom. She slowly went back to her office.

When she entered the Accounting Department Frances looked up at her and said, "Jesus, Carmen, are you all right?"

"Yes, I am fine." Carmen answered, "I just have a really upset stomach. I must have eaten something that did not agree with me."

"What was that?" Susan said, "A bad dose of shit-head?"

Carmen didn't answer. She just went to her desk and sat looking away from the other two girls. As usual they just looked at each other, shrugged their shoulders, and went back to work.

Lazarus dialed Woo's number and when the phone was answered said, "I think we have a problem. I am going to be busy the rest of the week. I have things to check on. Be at my place Tuesday at six thirty."

CHAPTER 12

Doris pulled her car into the parking lot at eight thirty on Wednesday morning, humming to herself. Yesterday had been uneventful, and though she felt that something had been missing, she just couldn't put her finger on it. She got out of her car in what appeared to be a very good mood, when she heard a voice say, "Getting ready for a really good day?"

Recognizing Robert Cleary's voice, she turned around and said, "It's going to be such a good day, and not even you can spoil it. And don't try to prove me wrong. Do you always get to work at eight thirty?"

"Yeah," he said, "I like to keep tabs on who comes in early and who comes in late."

"Always at exactly eight thirty?" Doris asked again.

"Always on the dot. Not a minute earlier. Not a minute later. You can set your watch on it." He said with a big grin on his face. "Why, are you planning on coming in at eight thirty, too?"

"No," Doris looked up at him smiling, "I plan on coming in at eight fifteen." At that, Doris turned and started walking toward the Stylex building.

Robert, walking behind Doris called out, "Maybe I'll start coming in at eight fifteen, too. Give me a chance to catch up on a lot of work. Thanks for the suggestion." He continued following Doris, a big smile on his face. Doris continued walking, shaking her head back and forth, otherwise ignoring Robert.

When Doris got into her office, Alice and Robin were already there, papers covering the desks, chairs, and half the floor.

"Whoa," Doris said, "Did you two spend the night here?"

"Almost," Alice said.

"I couldn't sleep," broke in Robin, "I'd been thinking of changes I wanted to make before you started reviewing the proposal. I got here

66

at five and called Alice to come in. She got here at six. I told her she could leave early Friday. I hope that's alright, Doris?"

"Certainly, that's fine." Doris answered. "Wait, I want you to stay until the Friday meeting is over. If the meeting lasts longer then I think, you can take off early any day you want next week. Is that OK?"

"Sure." Alice said, "That will be fine."

As Doris started walking toward her desk, Robin said, "I'll be ready for you by ten o'clock, Doris."

Meanwhile, Robert got to his office and when he entered, Bea, who was sitting at her desk, did not look up or greet him.

"Good morning, Bea," Robert said rather loudly, "Did you have a good day yesterday?"

When Bea didn't answer he continued, "Well I am glad to hear it. Try not to let anyone in to see me today. I have a report I have to work on and I need some quiet." He turned and went to his office door. When he opened the door, a command to stop was shouted at him by Bea. "What, Bea?" Robert said and turned to look at her, "Did you say something?"

Bea was sitting in her chair facing Robert, her hands on her hips when she said, "OK, Robert, are you going to tell me what's going on or do I have to go see George myself to get an answer? You know I hate not knowing what's going on."

"Bea," Robert started, "you are turning into my Aunt Bea right before my eyes. Come into my office, and I'll tell you what you want to know."

Bea jumped up and followed Robert into his office, shutting the door behind her. She sat on the edge of the chair in front of his desk. Robert sat in his chair and leaned back. "OK," he said, "I am going to tell you where we went yesterday. You must agree, if you tell anyone else about this it will be OK for me to kill you."

"Yes, yes, Robert," Bea said. "Now tell me, what's going on."

Robert told her the whole story about manufacturing and building on site homes. He related that George was considering buying in to a factory and creating new developments in the states around here."

"Remember, you're taking this to the grave, Bea," warned Robert. "If this gets out, I'll know it's you, and then I'll just have to let slip some rumors of my own, my lovely aunt."

Bea walked to the door, opened it, turned, and said, "I'm not worried, I'm just going to tell everyone you've got the hots for that Wilcox woman." She walked out and closed the door.

"Wait a minute, wait a minute," Robert shouted. His door snapped open and he shouted at Bea, "What are you talking about? I can't stand that woman. What kind of crazy talk is that? She is a swift pain. Don't you start any kind of talk. I don't care if you are dating the boss. I'll fire your ass out of here in a minute if you start something like that."

Bea sat down, looked at Robert, and smiled, "Oh, there must be something going on there." She turned to her desk and without looking at Robert said, "You better get in your office and write your report. And remember, you have been invited to a meeting Friday at one o'clock with," and here she sang the name, "Doris."

Robert walked back into his office and slammed the door. Bea sat there with a big smile on her face. "Gotta love women's intuition!" She said.

Robert spent the rest of the day in his office with papers spread over his desk writing his report, and interrupting his work periodically by yelling through the closed door, "Bea, coffee." Each time Bea brought the coffee in and put it on Robert's desk he mumbled, "Thanks," never looking up at her. And each time she left humming softly to herself, trying not to laugh out loud.

Meanwhile, Doris and Brenda were going over the presentation; rearranging the advertising, changing the focus, and deciding the order in which they were going. All the while Brenda defended her ideas. They only stopped to quickly eat the sandwiches Alice brought them for lunch. At three o'clock Doris said, "Brenda, you have done a great job. I think the meeting Friday will be a great success. Now, why don't you get with the agency and give them a heads up so everything will be ready for the meeting Friday afternoon?"

At four thirty Robert got up from his desk, walked out to Bea, and put fourteen pages of notes on her desk. This is a rough draft. Can I have it ready to review tomorrow morning?"

Bea looked at Robert, and then at the stack of papers he put on her desk, and then back to Robert, and said, "Even though it's four thirty and even though I will have to work all night to get your report ready, I will have it done by six in the morning for you to review.

"That will be fine. Thank you for your sacrifice," Robert answered, then walked to the door and said, "But, if you have it ready by eleven tomorrow, it will be good enough. We wouldn't want you to work your little fingers to the bone all night long." After a pause he said, "What made you think I have something for that woman?"

"Well," Bea answered, "you were examining her personnel file. You never examined my personnel file. There must be something going on."

"I don't believe it," Robert said. "BMB, that means big mouth Bea, that's what I am going to call you. And I didn't look at her file. You wouldn't let me. So just forget it."

Later, Robert walked out, went to the parking lot and when he got to his car looked over at Doris's car, shook his head, and left.

At five o'clock Doris got up, thanked Robin and Alice for a good job, and said, "Come on, let's get out of here. Tomorrow is another day. Oh, Robin, did you get those purchasing agents names?"

Robin answered, "Yes, I'll put them on your desk in the morning."

"Thanks. I'm gone." Doris said and left. When she got to the parking lot she looked at the empty space next to her car, smiled, and said to herself, "Early arrival, and early departure. I'll have to talk to you about this." She looked over to the other side of the parking lot and again, saw the same truck sitting all alone. She started to walk over to the truck, changed her mind, got into her car and drove off.

CHAPTER 13

As Doris approached the driveway into the Stylex parking lot, she looked at her watch, which showed eight twenty. *"Oh good,"* she thought, *"If he decides to come in at eight fifteen he's already here, and if he still plans on eight thirty then I am early. I can't have him thinking I time my arrival just to see him."* As she pulled into the lot, she saw Robert get out of his car and look straight at her as she pulled into a parking spot. As she got out of her car he was standing, waiting for her.

"What? Are you following me?" Doris said.

"What are you talking about?" Robert said, "I was here first. I think you have been following me. Can't keep away from my manly charm?"

Doris ignoring the last question said, "I thought you were coming in at eight fifteen. Remember, you were going to get some work done because you are always leaving early."

"I couldn't get here early. I had to take my kids to school this morning. And what happened about your coming to work at eight fifteen or did you forget?"

"No I didn't forget. I was just trying to avoid you." Doris said and walked away.

"Tomorrow at eight fifteen for sure," Robert called to her back and waited for Doris to get a head start before he followed, watching approvingly as she walked to the building.

Doris walked into her office, slammed her pocketbook down on Alice's desk and said, "Where's the coffee?"

"What's wrong, Doris?" Alice asked as Robin looked on.

Doris fumed, "He always comes in at eight thirty. I got here ten minutes early and the idiot pulls in right in front of me. He's so full of himself you could scream. Where's some coffee?" Doris marched into her office.

"The coffee is on your desk, Doris," Alice answered, "and the idiot must be Robert."

The only answer Alice got was a scream from Doris, "Where's my purse? What did I do with my damn purse?"

Robin walked in and put Doris's purse on her desk and said, "Do I get the distinct impression that you met Robert in the parking lot and had a little discussion with him?"

Doris picked up her coffee and said, "Oh, leave me alone." Robin turned, walked out of the office, shrugged her shoulders at Alice, and went to her desk.

A few minutes later Doris came to her door and spoke to both Alice and Robin, "So, who do I grovel and apologize to first? I'm sorry I made such an ass of myself, but he really infuriates me with his superior attitude."

"All is forgiven," Robin said, "but from now on, Alice or I will meet you in the parking lot and escort you into the building. We can save on coffee and getting yelled at."

Doris smiled and said, "Alright, one for your side. Where's Brenda?"

Alice answered, "Brenda's at the ad agency. She'll be back at noon. She would like to meet with you to go over the presentation."

"Send her in here when she's ready," Doris said, and returned to her office.

Robert went into his office and saw Bea with her back to the door typing furiously from the notes on the stack of papers Robert had given her the afternoon before. He quietly closed the door and softly said, "Good morning, Bea. How are you this fine morning?"

Bea turned around to look at Robert, smiled, and said, "What a fine mood you're in this morning, Robert. You must have already given someone a hard time to be so happy. Who was the poor victim?" Then thought, *"I'd bet my breakfast he ran into Doris less than 5 minutes ago!"*

"There is no poor victim. I didn't give anyone a hard time. Where is my report?"

71

"You said by eleven o'clock. It won't be ready a minute before. Now leave me alone, or it won't be done until noon."

Susan, Carmen, and Frances were sitting at their desks in the accounting office when Stanley Woo came in, went over to Carmen's desk, leaned over, and whispered, "If I find out you were the one that told Lazarus about Dragon and Tiger, I am going to fire your ass right out of here. I don't care what Lazarus says." Woo then straightened up and walked out.

Carmen sat very still taking large gulps of breath, all color drained from her face, and perspiration ran down her forehead. Susan quickly walked over to Carmen asking, "My God, Carmen, are you alright? You look like you are going to faint. What did Woo say to you to upset you so much? What is going on with you? I'm going to tell Deana. You look like you've seen a ghost."

Frances walked over and added, "Carmen, tell us what's wrong. You look like you're going to have a heart attack."

"He just wanted a list of receivables." Carmen answered, "I'm having trouble at home and it keeps bothering me. There is nothing going on here. Please stay out of my business, and please don't tell Deana anything. I don't want to get fired."

***

At a quarter past twelve Brenda rushed into her office with an arm full of folders about fourteen inches square and announced to Alice and Robin, "I am ready. Where is Doris?"

Alice answered, "In her office eagerly awaiting you."

Brenda walked to Doris's office door, which was slightly ajar, pushed it open with her arms full of the folders, and said, "Are you ready?"

Doris looked up, smiled, and answered, "Let's get going. Call Robin and Alice in here. We can use them as an audience to see how we do."

Brenda went back to the door and said, "Robin, Alice, come in here. You are the first guinea pigs for our big shot at the big shots. Ask as many questions as you can."

72

Brenda spent the next hour going over the type and size of the ads, what markets they were going to target, the type of periodicals in which the ads were going to run, the best days for the ads to appear, and the results they were looking to accomplish. At the end, the three women applauded, and Brenda took several bows, when Doris said, "That was great, Brenda. Now after I give a short introductory statement of what our goals are, you are going to make the same presentation you just made."

Brenda, with her mouth open and her eyes wide, looked at Doris and didn't answer for a full minute. Then she gave a sigh and a little laugh and said, "Wow, Doris, you had me going for a while. I really thought you were serious."

Doris smiled and answered back, "I am very serious. You did a really great job in answering all our questions. No one can present your work better than you can. Now let's go down to the cafeteria and get some lunch, if they are not already closed."

"Oh, God, Doris," Brenda said, "Are you sure? I never did anything like this before."

"Brenda, you just did it. You will be perfect. Let's see if we can eat," Doris said as she got up and headed for the door. The three girls followed her out to the cafeteria.

At the same time Robert finished reading the report given to him by Bea, came out of his office, and said, "Bea, great job. Come on, I'm taking you out to lunch today, that is, if you don't already have a date."

"Robert, the cafeteria is free," she replied, ignoring the last statement.

"Well, come on anyway. I want to talk about some changes I need to make to this report." Robert said.

"OK, Robert, last of the big spenders, you can buy me lunch in the cafeteria. But don't get friendly." Bea answered as she got up, picked up her purse, and followed Robert out the door.

Robert and Bea approached the cafeteria from one end of the hallway. Doris and her group approached from the other. Both groups met at the main doorway.

"Good afternoon, ladies," Robert crooned, "How did you know that I always eat lunch here at this time?"

"Why, Robert," Robin crooned back, "We all know what time you come to lunch. We even know what time you come to work. Don't we, girls?" Robin turned and winked at Doris. Brenda and Alice, turned back, nodded at Bea, and led the three into the cafeteria ahead of Robert and Bea.

"What was that all about?" asked Bea.

"Please don't even ask." Robert answered as they followed the other women into the serving line.

The two groups were the only ones in line, with Doris first and Robin last, then Bea and Robert. The three women seemed to ignore Robert and Bea and took a table at the far side of the cafeteria.

Later, Doris, Brenda and Robin had several more practice sessions going over the presentations for the big meeting Friday. After the last rehearsal Brenda looked at her watch and said, "Quarter to six. Can we call it quits?"

"Good idea", said Doris, "let's get out of here."

When they got to the parking lot, theirs were the last three cars remaining, except for the truck at the far end of the parking lot.

Doris said, "Whose truck is that?"

Brenda answered, "Oh, that's Forman's truck. I wonder what he is doing here so late."

"You know, I think he is following me." Doris said. "I seem to be running into Forman all the time. He is starting to creep me out."

"I don't know, Doris." Robin said, "But if it makes you uncomfortable, why don't you talk to Joe Everton. He will know what to do."

"Good idea," said Doris, "Let's worry about it after the meeting."

The ladies got in their respective cars and left. Shortly after they left, the truck pulled out of the parking lot.

CHAPTER 14

Friday was the big day for Doris and Brenda, the day of the first presentation outlining the new marketing and advertising direction the company would be taking. Hopefully that is, if everything went as well as Doris hoped. Today Doris did arrive at eight fifteen, and thankfully there was no Robert to hassle her. When she arrived at her office, Brenda, Robin, and Alice were already sitting at their desks drinking coffee and reviewing the presentation. Doris laughed, "Looks like an early start. What's going on?"

Handing Doris a cup of coffee, Alice said, "They are driving me crazy. I have changed the first page twice, the second page once, and the third page three times, and they haven't finished going over the fourth page yet."

Doris pulled up a chair alongside Brenda's desk and asked, "What kind of changes are we making to the presentation? I thought you did a great job yesterday."

"It's nothing major, just cleaning up a few things," Brenda said, handing the pages to Doris. "I just keep reviewing the proposal and getting some of the bugs out."

Doris laughed, "Putting in commas and taking out commas is really just cleaning up." Putting the pages down Doris turned to Alice. "Alice, would you go down to the cafeteria and get more coffee and a dish of pastry? We are not going to eat lunch before the meeting so let's just all have a party and relax." Doris looked at Brenda and added, "Well, let's relax as much as possible".

Alice came back with the coffee and pastry and the girls settled down around Brenda's desk. Doris began, "As long as we're relaxing, we might as well take the opportunity to get to know each other a little more. I have two girls, Mary is six, and Susan is three. My husband was an air force pilot. He was killed three years ago, right after Susan was born, in an air accident. I tried dating a couple of times, but as soon as it began getting to the next level, I called it off. My folks live in a retirement village out West. And that's it."

Nothing was said for a few seconds and then Alice started. "I am married to an electrician for four years. I have a one year old daughter. My father died nine months ago, and my mother came to live with us to take care of my daughter so I could go back to work. This job gives us a lot of extra income. We are saving to buy a house. Robin, your next."

"Well," Robin said, "I hooked up with a guy for what I thought was going to be forever in my last year at college. We lasted three years, although, I couldn't get him to commit. 'When the time is right' was the answer I got. But it was going great. When I came home a day early from an out of town meeting I had with the marketing firm I was with, I found my loving boyfriend in bed loving some other girl. That was about a year ago, and I haven't met anyone I am interested in trying. You know what I mean?"

"Yeah, I know," said Brenda, "But you know what? I am twice as dumb as you are. The same thing happened to me twice. The first one was five years older than me, and I found him with someone ten years older than he was. The kicker was she was rich. The second time I was careful and got one that was forty years old, which was ten years older than I was. This one had a little money. Guess what? The son of a bitch decided, with a little money, he could get an eighteen year old bimbo, with boobs that went on forever, and rocks in her head for brains."

Everyone laughed and they then spent the next three hours trashing men, except of course, Alice's husbands. Finally Doris, looking at her watch said, "It's time to shine."

Brenda got up, gathered up her folders, and without saying anything led the way out of the office, and up the stairs to the conference room.

Doris and Robin sat down at the conference table. Brenda put her folders in front of the chair next to Doris and set mock ups of ads on the easel next to her chair. Joseph Everton and Stanley Horworth came in followed by Brenton Lazarus, Dietmar Wertzer, and Clarence Lucci. The men positioned themselves facing Doris and the other two women. Deana Zimmer came in and sat down between Stanley Horworth and Brenton Lazarus. The group around the table was engaged in small talk until Doris, looking at her watch, said, "Well I guess we're ready to start."

Clarence Lucci interrupted, "Robert will be here in a minute."

"Robert?" Doris asked. "Oh you mean Robert Cleary. Well, we can bring him up to speed if he comes in later."

Before Doris could start, Robert boomed into the room, "Sorry I'm late. Unavoidably detained." He looked around, smiled at Doris, sat down next to Clarence, and in a horse whisper said, "Did I miss anything important?"

"No, Robert," Doris answered his question, "We waited just for you."

"Oh, thank you," Robert shot back. "That was just so sweet of you."

At that Robert slumped back in his seat and waited. Doris, a steely look in her eyes, began the presentation. She explained the direction of the new advertising campaign, how it was going to target home improvement stores and contractors, and even go after the do-it-yourself group of people, especially for the closet systems. Brenda will now go over our proposed ads and the markets we wish to build.

"I've got a question for you," Lazarus said in his normal abrasive tone.

"Yes, Brenton?" Doris said with a smile on her face. "What question did you wish to ask?"

Lazarus started, "Why is all this necessary? Robert, here, is keeping us pretty busy with his salesmen. If we hired more salesmen, instead of spending money on ads trying to convince some old bunch of ladies to get their houses fixed up, we would have so much work; we would have to outsource our production overseas. We would save tons of money, and the company would be so profitable George would be doubling everyone's bonus." By the end of his speech, Brenton was talking very loud and seem to be addressing Joseph Everton instead of Doris.

Before Doris could answer Robert said, "Hold on, Brenton. This may not be such a bad idea. After all, the builders we have are loyal followers of Stylex. This leaves my guys free to extend the market. This will just give us added exposure and will make contacting new builders even easier."

Lazarus, giving Robert and Doris dirty looks, sat down and started drawing "x's" on the pad of paper in front of him.

Doris stood looking at Robert, her mouth hanging open a little bit in utter surprise at his defense of her proposals.

"Oh, er, yes, as I was saying, Brenda will present the next section of the presentation."

Brenda got up and spent the next forty minutes explaining how the target markets were picked and where the ads were going to be placed. Everyone was listening and occasionally making notes. Everyone, except Brenton, who continued to make "x's" on his pad in the shape of trees, cars, or airplanes.

At the end Doris got up and said, "Gentlemen and lady, does anyone have any questions?"

At this, Brenton got up and walked out of the room. Some of the men just shook their heads. Robert raised his hand and said, "Yes, I have several questions." Robert did not sound angry or hostile, but more concerned with Stylex sales. He continued, "When will these ads run? Will they run in all markets at the same time? How can I schedule my men to make sales calls to these home improvement stores without interfering with their sales calls to their new prospective builder clients?"

"The ads won't start for about six weeks. They will run sequentially around the areas we targeted. Some ad schedules may run overlapping in some areas. As for your salesmen's schedules, I would like to propose some ideas to you. I don't think it is necessary to handle the details while all these good people just sit around. I would like to end the meeting now, if there are no more questions. I can get together with you later today, if you have time."

Everyone got up spouting compliments about the presentation and left. The three women stood in the room and looked at each other.

"Good job, Brenda. You were great." Doris said.

Brenda answered, "Thanks, Doris. Wow, I did do pretty well. And I understand Brenton's response, but, what about that Robert?"

Doris smiled, "I'll tell you the truth; you could have knocked me over with a feather. I thought Robert was going to make the speech that the idiot Lazarus made. I just don't understand that man, one minute he thinks my job is a waste of time, and the next minute I'm the best thing that happened around here. I just don't understand that man."

"We'll see how he feels about entertaining twenty purchasing agents in the next six weeks. Then you'll really see how he feels about you." Brenda said.

"But first, let's get some lunch," Doris said. All the files were picked up and they started out the door.

After lunch, they went back to their office. Doris picked up the list of purchasing agents that Alice put on her desk and waved to the group as she walked out of the office. The girls shouting "Good Luck" followed her out and she thought, *"Right into the lions den."* She walked to Robert's office and said to no one, "Why am I nervous? And why is my stomach acting up? I hope I didn't get food poisoning from the cafeteria."

CHAPTER 15

Doris entered the office greeting Bea, "Hi, Bea is Robert busy? I need to see him for a half hour."

Bea looked up and smiled, "Hi, Doris. How did the meeting go?" And without waiting for an answer continued, "Just go on in. He's not busy."

"Thanks, Bea. I thought the meeting went surprisingly well," Doris said, and turned toward Robert's closed door and knocked.

"What?" Robert screamed.

Doris opened the door and said, "Excuse me, Robert, Bea said you were not busy and for me to come in. Of course, I wouldn't dream of coming in without first knocking, and being invited in, and hopefully, asked to sit down"

Robert stood up, smiled and said, "Please come into my office, Doris. And Doris, please sit in this chair next to my desk."

Doris sat, smiled at Robert, and started, "First, I want to thank you for coming to the defense of my presentation. I thought…"

Robert held up his hand, "I don't like your proposal of changing the direction of Stylex. I just didn't like Brandon spouting off like that. Actually, that was what I was going to say."

The smile left Doris's face. She sat looking at Robert for a few seconds before continuing. "Well then, I withdraw the thanks. And if that is the way you feel, I don't think there will be any need to continue this meeting."

"Well, why don't you give it a try anyway," Robert said, "I pride myself on being a reasonable person. If you can convince me that your proposals will help Stylex, then I might consider getting on board with you."

Doris sat considering her chances of success with getting Robert to entertain the list of purchasing agents she held in her hand. Shaking her head up and down she said, "OK, Robert, if you are a reasonable person, and haven't already made up your mind, I will."

Doris was interrupted by a knock on the door. The door opened and Bea walked into the room carrying a tray of coffee, cream, and sugar. She placed the tray on the desk and said, "I thought this meeting might last a while, so I brought coffee. Doris, I didn't know how you wanted your coffee so I brought cream and sugar." Bea winked at Robert and walked out.

Doris called her thanks, then put the cream and one sugar in her cup of coffee and continued, "If you haven't already made up your mind that you are against everything I am suggesting; I would like to ask a favor of you."

Doris waited for an answer and Robert sat quietly looking at her. Then he leaned forward and without breaking eye contact said, "I tell you what. I am going to do anything you want. I will not say anything against your ideas. You will have my full cooperation. There is, however, one stipulation."

Doris started shaking her head back and forth, color rising in her checks, and Robert continued, "That stipulation is that you have nine months to show some strong results. If nothing happens, I will tell George and Joe to save a lot of money and go back to the way things were."

"Oh," Doris said, "I thought." Doris stopped and smiled at Robert saying, "That is a fair stipulation. In nine months, I feel Stylex sales will double, that is, if production can keep up. Now, the first thing I want you to do is to invite this list of purchasing agents," Doris lay the list in front of Robert, "to see the factory and talk to you about selling Stylex products. They will be flown here at our expense, one evening, spend the next morning with you, have lunch with you and hopefully with either George or Joe and then fly home that afternoon. I would like to see you invite four at a time."

Doris sat back and watched Robert as he sat, still looking right into her eyes. After a few seconds, which seemed like minutes to Doris, she said, "Well, you said you would do anything I wanted."

Robert, still looking directly into Doris's eyes handed the list back to Doris, said, "You have beautiful eyes. Starting a week from this Monday, I want you to invite four from your list. I will meet them at the hotel Monday evening for drinks. I will pick them up Tuesday morning, bring them here and show them around, make a good sales pitch, try to get a commitment from each one of them, get either George or Joe to join us for lunch, and then drive them to the airport for their flights home. And, you really do have beautiful eyes."

Doris, red faced, said, "Thank you, Robert for meeting with these purchasing agents. I will arrange the first four to arrive a week from this Monday. I will give Bea the information."

Doris got up, turned, walked to the door, turned around, and looked at Robert who was now standing. She walked back to the desk, picked up her cup of coffee, and walked out the door without saying anything further.

After Doris left, Bea went into Robert's office and smiled, "Well," she said, "How did the meeting go, Darling?"

Robert shot back, "Oh, shut up. Get me some hot coffee. And close the door behind you."

Bea left the room and in a minute was back with a cup of steaming hot coffee. She placed the cup in front of Robert and said, "You know, she really is cute. And she has beautiful eyes."

Robert looking up, said, "Have you been listening at the door?"

Bea answered, "No, of course not. Oh, Robert, you didn't tell her she had beautiful eyes did you? That's like saying you're in love."

"Listen very closely," Robert said, his eyes narrowed and his mouth in a straight line, "I really don't like that woman. She is a busy body. I really can't stand her. And telling her she has pretty eyes does not mean I love her. Now, is there anything about what I just said that you do not understand?"

"OK, Robert," Bea said, "I apologize that I told you that you loved her." And with that Bea walked out the door, a very big smile on her face.

Back in accounting, Carmen picked up the phone after the first ring as usual, and with no preamble heard, "I will be out of town until Monday night. Be there at six o'clock on Tuesday. And don't be a minute late. Do you understand? Don't be a minute late."

Before Carmen could say a word the phone went dead.

CHAPTER 16

After a quiet weekend of playing with the girls and cleaning the house with Margaret's help, Doris felt ready for work. Not wanting to meet Robert in the parking lot, she deliberately came in a little late, arriving at a quarter to nine. The only parking space she found open was next to the sidewalk in front of the building. When walking to the building, she noticed Robert's car nearby. *"Well, he got here early this morning. I will have to congratulate him,"* she thought. When she opened the office door, Alice was busy typing, while Brenda and Robin were busy arranging ads on the conference desk. Doris started, "Boy, it looks likes things are really humming around here. Sorry I'm a little late. Have you arranged all the ads?"

Alice jumped up, "I'll get the coffee, Doris. We're almost finished with everything you wanted."

"Come sit down. We are ready for you." Brenda said as she sat down with a stack of papers in front of her.

They spent the next three hours going over the home improvement ads of competitors in newspapers in all the areas Stylex had been selling its products. Periodically, Doris would tell Alice to, "make a note of that," or, "I want to discuss this with Joe." At twelve thirty Doris looked at her watch and said, "Gosh girls, isn't anyone hungry? I'm starved."

Robin laughed, "Doris, we've been sticking our tongues out at each other for the past hour. You were so intent, we didn't want to break up your train of thought"

"Well, the only thing I can think of now is food. Let's go." And with this they all stood up and headed for the door.

When they opened the door, Forman was standing in the hallway. When he saw Doris he smiled, gave a small wave with his hand, and walked away.

"He is making me more and more nervous. I seem to see him all over the place." Doris whispered. "Is he always around here?"

Robin whispered back, "It is pretty strange. He usually never leaves the factory. Maybe he just likes you Doris."

They all shrugged and headed for the cafeteria. When they entered there was a small line at the serving counter. People were already starting to carry their trays to the dirty tray cart and leaving.

As they stood in line, Robert came up behind them holding his tray with dirty dishes and said, "Well, I thought you girls found a better place to eat."

Before any of the others could say anything Doris spoke, a condescending smile on her face "Robert, I understand you are such a connoisseur of food that nobody would think of eating any place else but where you eat."

"Well, Doris," Robert said, "Thank you for the compliment. It's so sweet of you. Please try the meatloaf and mashed potatoes. They are excellent." With that, he smiled and walked off.

"Well," Brenda said, "I don't know who got the better of that little exchange. Doris, you better keep practicing, or he may end up being nice."

They all laughed and turned back to the serving line. Doris turned her head slightly to see Robert leave the cafeteria.

After lunch the four girls returned and resumed their ad discussion. At two o'clock Doris said, "OK, I've got enough to go see Joe." She picked up the phone and dialed. Grace answered the phone, "Joe Everton's office, Grace speaking."

Doris answered back, "Hi, Grace, it's Doris. Can I get in to see your father – I mean Joe – sometime this afternoon?"

Grace laughed, "Doris, I have the same problem. I can't call him father here, and I have a hard time calling my father by his first name. Aside from that, hold on a minute, and I'll see what his plans are." A few minutes later Grace was back on the phone, "He asked if four thirty would be good."

Doris answered back, "Tell him that four thirty is fine as long as he doesn't mind working a little overtime."

Grace laughed, "I'll tell him. See you at four thirty." And with that, they both hung up the phone.

The girls split up. Doris going back to her office, Brenda and Robin to their desks, and Alice to her desk where she started typing up the notes she took.

Doris called her house and left a message, "Margaret, I'm going to be working late tonight. Please bathe and feed the girls. I should be home by seven thirty or so."

***

Back in the factory, Bill Bernard opened up Forman's office door, "Hey, Forman, can I see you for a minute?"

Forman looked up, waved his huge hand, and said, "Sure, Bill, what's up?"

Bill Bernard came into the office, sat down, and proceeded to tell Forman about the meeting he had with Lazarus and Woo. At the end he said, "I would like to talk to Mr. Stillwell. What do you think I should do?"

Forman's chair groaned under the weight as he leaned back. "Well," he said, "first, I think you better not call George, Mr. Stillwell. He likes the first name thing. Second, I definitely think you should talk to him. And, you are right about not talking to him in his office." Forman picked up the phone and dialed a number. When the phone answered he said, "George, I have Bill Bernard here in my office. He just told me an interesting story that I think you should hear. I don't think this is an in the office type of meeting." There was a pause and he continued, "Tomorrow night, eight o'clock, at your house. OK, I'll give him directions. He will be at your house at eight. Turning to Bill he said, "You know where he lives, don't you?" Bill nodded his head yes, and Forman continued. "You were right not discussing this with anyone. Go see George. He will tell you what to do."

"Thanks, Forman," Bill said and walked out of the office.

Forman waited a few minutes and redialed the number. "George," he said, when the phone was answered, "I think we should put an end to this. I can take care of this for you. No one will be the wiser."

"Listen, Forman," George said, "We will do this my way. Do you understand me? We will do it my way. You have got to promise me."

"Alright, George, your way. I promise." He hung up the phone, slowly shook his head, put his hands together and cracked his knuckles. The sound was like gunshots.

CHAPTER 17

At four thirty Doris was at Joe Everton's office. She was greeted by Grace and shown into Joe's office.

Grace said in a clipped tone, "Joe, Doris is here."

Joe looked up and said, "Thank you, Grace. Come in Doris."

Doris smiled, went to the front of the desk, and sat in the chair, putting the folder she was holding on the desk.

Joe Everton called out, "Grace, you can go on home. We will probably be here a while.

Well Doris, how are things going? That was a very nice presentation. I'm sorry Brenton was so negative. But, I was happy to see Robert stick up for you. I guess you really won him over."

"I was a little surprised at that myself," Doris started, "When I thanked Robert, he told me he was going to say the same thing. He just didn't want Brenton on my case. I hope I am not this unpopular with everyone."

Joe leaned forward, "Listen, Doris, you are the new kid on the block. I wouldn't worry about Brenton. He has issues himself which I cannot discuss right now. As for Robert, I want you to believe me, no matter what he says, Robert likes everyone. He can be tough sometimes, but, he will always stick up for anyone that's seems to be in trouble. And that's just what he did at the meeting. When Brenton attacked you, Robert was the first to come to your aid."

"You know something, Joe, when I look back on it, it does seem you are right. Now, I want to discuss my specific plans and see what you think."

After two hours of discussion, Doris got up, picked up her folder, and thanked Joe. She left his office and went back down to hers. She sat at her desk for a half hour making additional notes. She looked at her watch, which read five past seven, closed her file, and put it into her drawer. She locked the drawer, picked up her purse, and walked out.

Doris left the building and started walking to her car. Looking around, she saw the parking lot was empty except for her car and the same truck parked at the back of the lot. As she approached her car, another car pulled up to the sidewalk. Three men got out and started walking toward Doris' car. She looked at them, one blonde and two dark haired men. All three appeared to be muscular and walked with an arrogance that made Doris nervous. They arrived at Doris' car the same time she did.

"Can I help you with something?" Doris asked.

The blonde man pulled a switchblade from his side, flipped it open, and held it in front of him. The other two men went to either side of Doris, surrounding her.

The blonde man said, "Why, sweet cheeks, we want you to come for a little ride with us. We just want to tell you how pretty you look."

The other two men grabbed Doris and started pulling her to their car. Doris went limp causing one man to lose hold of her arm. She quickly stood up and hit the other man in the face. Before she could pull her other arm free, she was again grabbed and the two men stood holding her. The blonde man came close and put the knife to Doris's face. "If you don't come quietly, I will make hamburger of your pretty face. Understand?"

Before they could start moving again, they heard a screech of tires and the truck that was at the other side of the parking lot stopped next to them. The blonde man turned around as Forman leapt from the truck. The blonde man stepped forward and swung his knife at Forman. Forman put up his arm to block the knife jab. The knife went through Forman's lower left arm. Forman did not seem to notice. He stepped forward and drove his fist into the man's rib cage. A whoosh of air came out of the man's mouth as Forman's fist broke several of the man's ribs.

The men holding Doris pushed her down and each one pulled out a knife. Forman stepped into the man closest to him and hit him in the face before the man could raise his knife. The other man swung his knife at Forman. Forman caught his hand and brought his other hand down on the man's arm breaking it so the bones stuck out through the skin. The man started to sink to the ground, but Forman put his hand around the man's neck, stood him up, and slammed him against the truck. He slowly brought his fist back aiming for the man's face when Doris got up and screamed, "No! Albert no! Albert, no, no! Don't hit him! Please don't hit him!" Forman froze. Doris in a quieter voice said, "Albert, please let the man down."

Forman slowly released the hold on the man's throat. He slowly sank to the ground. He turned to Doris. He quickly went over to her, picked her up by the arms, and gently placed her on the hood of her car. "Are you hurt?" he asked, "I should have been closer. I am so sorry Doris, I should have been closer."

"Albert," Doris said, "You saved my life. Thank you." And then Doris saw the knife sticking out of Forman's arm. She screamed, "Albert, you've been stabbed! Oh, my God, Albert, you're hurt!"

Forman looked down at the knife in his arm and smiled at Doris, "It's nothing, Doris. Just a few stitches. We can't take it out now. It'll just bleed faster."

Just then, two men came running from the building and at the same time sirens were heard coming closer. As the two men were running, one called out, "Forman, are you OK?"

Forman nodded his head up and down and answered back, "Don't let these guys here get away." The men came to a halt between the truck and the car, looked at the three men lying on the ground and laughed.

"Forman, they won't be conscious for a couple of days. What happened?" the other man asked.

Doris answered, "They tried to kidnap me. If Albert hadn't come along, I would have been a goner."

When Doris said the name Albert, both men took two steps back and nervously watched Forman. When he didn't seem to react, the men relaxed. Just then, two police cars arrived with lights flashing. One policeman got out of each car with guns drawn. Both men raised their hands and backed up revealing Doris and Forman.

Doris yelled, "Wait, Officers, Albert was helping me. These men on the ground were trying to kidnap me."

Forman nodded to the police officers, "Hello, Pete, Frank, I am sorry about this.

"Hello, Forman," the officer called Pete said, "Did you leave any of them alive for us?"

Doris looked at the one called Pete and asked, "Do you know Albert?"

Pete took a quick look at Forman, poised to run if necessary. When Forman didn't move Pete answered, "Oh, yes I certainly do. Forman saved my life a while back. I will never forget him."

Just then an ambulance arrived. Two paramedics ran over carrying their medical bags. Pete yelled at the two medics, "Be careful. Don't move anybody. There are probably a lot of broken bones. And this guy," Pete pointed to Forman, "has a knife stuck in his arm."

The medics nodded, bent and checked out the three men lying on the ground. They went back to the ambulance and brought out three stretchers and with some difficulty managed to slide the three men onto the stretchers. They then wheeled them over and slid them into the ambulance.

Forman looked inside the ambulance and said, "I can drive myself to the hospital."

Forman got into his truck and started to pull out, when Doris rushed over and held up a hand to stop Forman from leaving. She looked up at him saying, "Albert, thank you for looking out for me. It was such a brave thing to do."

Forman shook his head and Doris saw tears running down his cheeks. The truck pulled away, and Doris just stood looking after the truck wondering if what she saw was real.

The police officer named Pete came over to Doris, "You will need to come down to the station and give a statement.

That was such a brave thing Albert did."

"You know," Pete said, "Every time you say Albert I get really nervous. He reacts really badly when someone calls him that."

"I don't understand that at all. He told me to call him Albert. He said he would like it if I called him that. You said he saved your life. What happened?"

Pete answered, "I was called to a disturbance in a store. When I walked in, these two guys with guns came out, took my gun, and told me I was going to be their ultimate sacrifice. They were going to kill me. Forman came over and one of the guys shot him in the shoulder. Before the guy got another shot off, Forman grabbed his hand with the gun and yanked it hard enough to pull his shoulder out of its socket. He backhanded the other guy in his neck, breaking it. That guy died. Forman was given an award, and made an honorary member of the police force. I think every cop in the city knows Forman. You are really lucky that he was here. Lord knows what would have happened, if you didn't have help."

Doris swayed and was steadied by Pete who said, "You want to go to the hospital first and let them check you over?"

"Oh, yes," Doris answered, "I want to check on Albert, I mean Forman, to see if he is alright. Will you bring me back to my car when we are done at the hospital?"

"Yeah," Pete answered, "That won't be a problem." He turned to the other policeman and said, "Frank, I'm taking the lady down to the hospital and then down to the station for a statement. Clean up this place and call a tow truck for their car." Without waiting for an answer, Pete took Doris by the elbow and led her over to the passenger side of the police car. He opened the door and let Doris sit down and swing her legs inside. He closed the door, went around the car, got in, and started the car. The drive to the hospital was done in silence.

When they arrived at the hospital, Doris asked to make a call home. When she reached Margaret she told her what happened and that she was unscathed. Then she asked at the admitting desk to see Albert Forman, but was told he was already released. She was then taken to the police department, where she told the secretary taking down what she said happened, that Forman stopped them from dragging her by knife point to their car. When that was over, Pete drove her back to the Stylex parking lot.

Doris got out, went to her car, got inside, and started the engine. Pete signaled her ahead of him and she drove away. Pete followed her all the way to her house. He waited until she had opened her door and waved to him before he pulled away.

CHAPTER 18

When Doris entered her house Margaret rushed to her and took her into a big hug, "Doris! I was so worried. Are you alright? What happened?"

Doris moved away from Margaret, but before she could answer she was engulfed in another hug from Anna. "Doris, I was so afraid for you. As soon as Bobby heard, he told me to come over and see if there was anything I could do. Margaret already took care of the girls. I don't know what I can do. Do you need anything? Is there anything I can do? Can Bobby do anything for you at work? Oh, Doris, I feel so awful for you. What happened?"

Doris pulled away and thanked Margaret and Anna saying, "I am completely fine. Just a sore behind from being pushed down. Thank God for Albert Forman. He's a man that works at the factory. He happened to be in the parking lot when these three men tried to drag me into their car. They all had these big knives, but Albert is a pretty big guy, and he just beat the three of them up. One of the policemen that showed up told me that this Albert Forman saved his life. I hope Albert is OK. One of the men stuck a knife right through his arm. He didn't even seem to notice it. He'd already left the hospital before I could see him. I have to go see him in the morning. I have the feeling he's been watching me. It was really making me feel uneasy, but now, I am sure glad he was there."

Anna, with tears rolling down her cheeks, had released Doris, and gasped, "How terrible. It was really lucky that man was there to help you."

Doris smiled at her and said, "Bobby told you to come over? How did Bobby know about this?"

"Doris, remember, he works with you at Stylex. Bea thought it funny that you didn't put the two names, Robert and Bobby, together." Anna said, "He called, asking me come over to check and see if you needed anything." Doris, standing there absorbing the Robert and Bobby thing, looked up at Anna saying, "There is really nothing I need.

I really appreciate your coming over, and I will thank Robert for sending someone to check on me."

"Oh," Anna said, "if you are alright, then OK. But I don't know what would have happened if this Albert Forman guy hadn't been there."

Doris said, "I was really lucky he was there."

As soon as Doris stopped talking, there was a knock at the front door. When Margaret opened the door Bea Patterson rushed in, saw Doris, ran over, and gave her a hug. Bea pulled away holding Doris' arms and said, "I had to come over to see if you were alright and if I could do anything for you. Robert called and told me I should come over to see if you needed anything. Doris, take tomorrow off and rest up. I will tell the girls to cover for you. Is there anything else I can do?"

Bea looked around and saw Anna, who said, "Bea, I already asked DD. It looks like she has everything under control."

"Anna, Bea," Doris said, "I really appreciate your coming over. The support means a lot to me. I want you to thank Robert for sending both of you over. I guess he wouldn't have known what to say if he came himself."

Anna and Bea laughed in agreement and Bea said, "Get a good night's sleep. If you don't feel like coming in in the morning, that's OK. Anna and I will let you get to bed. Take good care of her, Margaret. Come on, Anna; let's let Doris get some rest."

Doris walked them to the door and thanked them again for coming. She closed the door and turning to Margaret said, "All I want to do is take a shower and get in bed."

"Don't you want me to make you anything to eat?" Margaret said. "I still have some supper left for you."

"No, I'm fine." Doris said, "Did the girls go to bed without any trouble?"

"I just told them that Mama had to work late. They were very good, as usual." Margaret answered.

Doris turned, walked to her bedroom, closed the door, and muttered to herself, "some night." She took a quick shower, got into bed, closed her eyes, and was asleep immediately.

***

Waking up to the alarm, Doris got out of bed and went right into the girl's room. They were both sleeping. Doris looked at them with satisfaction and love. She then bent down and kissed Mary several times until she opened her eyes. Doris then went to Susan and repeated the process. "OK, sleepy heads," she said, "It's time to get up. Who wants help first to get dressed?"

"I do!" Mary said without moving. "I want to get dressed first today."

Just then Margaret came in and said, "Who do I get to dress today?"

Susan said, "Me, dress me. But I want Mama to pick out my dress."

After the girls were dressed Margaret took them to the kitchen for breakfast while Doris got ready for work. Before she left she went to the kitchen, kissed the girls, and told Margaret that she would definitely be home for dinner.

Doris pulled into the parking lot and noticed a uniformed guard at the entrance to the lot who waved to her as she entered. She picked a place near the door to the office section of the building, looked around before she got out of her car, and noticed another uniformed guard in the middle of the lot. She got out of the car, locked it, and looked around for Robert's car. She did not see it. She walked directly to the factory entrance of the building.

Once inside, she immediately went to the door marked Forman. She went over and knocked. She was greeted by a loud "Come in." She entered to see Forman sitting at his desk with his forearm bandaged and with a huge stack of papers in front of him. When he saw Doris, he immediately stood up and said, "Good morning, Doris, I didn't know if you would be coming in this morning, after last night."

"Actually," Doris said, "I didn't think you would be in today, after being stabbed and all. I just came in to see if you were alright. And I wanted to talk to you for a few minutes, if you have the time."

"I have the time for you whenever you want, Doris," Forman said, "Please sit down. Do you want a cup of coffee?"

"No coffee, thanks," Doris said, "I want to ask you a bunch of questions. The first question is, why did you tell me to call you Albert? Every time I say your name everyone cringes expecting an explosion. The second question is, why have you been following me around? The last question is, why are you always in the parking lot waiting in your truck? I always see the truck in the parking lot. That was you, wasn't it?"

"Doris," Forman began, "I apologize for making you feel uncomfortable by following you around and waiting for you in the parking lot. Although, I certainly am glad I did. I want you to look at this. I think it will answer all your questions." Forman took a small picture out of his drawer. It was an old fashioned sepia toned photograph of a woman dressed in a nineteen twenties style dress and hat. Doris looked at the picture and saw herself in the picture. She looked up in surprise and said, "Albert, where did you get this picture of me dressed like this? I never had a dress like this on in my life. You are really scaring me, Albert."

Forman smiled at her. "Doris," he said, "That is not a picture of you. Look on the back. You see the date, nineteen twenty eight. That is a picture of my mother. I don't know how it could be, Doris, but you are exactly like my mother. The face, the hair, the body, the way you point your feet when you stand, you are a reincarnation of my mother. I was eight years old when my mother was murdered. She walked into a store that was being held up and the thief just shot her. I should have been with her. I maybe could have stopped her from being killed. I was always a big kid and pretty much not afraid of anything.

Growing up, the only person that called me Albert was my mother. Everyone called me Forman. If anyone called me Albert, I would really beat them up. Albert was only used by my mother for as long as I can remember. Having you call me Albert brought me back to the happiest days of my life. I won't allow anyone to call me Albert, except you. And that's why I watch over you. If anyone tries to hurt you, I will probably kill them, like I should have done to protect my mother. You realize you stopped me from killing that man last night. I felt my mother telling me not to hit him. No one else could have stopped me.

Doris looked up from the picture. Tears were running down her face. "Albert," she whispered, "I really am a duplicate of your mother. But, you couldn't have protected your mother in that situation. You were only a little boy." Doris smiled at him and continued, "Even a big little boy could not stop someone from shooting your mother. It wasn't your fault that she died. I am not your mother, but I certainly would like to be your friend. And you did save my life last night. I will be eternally grateful." Doris got up and Forman stood. Doris walked around the desk and hugged Forman, although, her hands only reached to his sides and her head rested against his chest. She stepped back, looked up at him and said, "I would be proud to continue to call you Albert, and thank you for looking out for me." I see they have two security guards in the parking lot now."

"Yeah," Forman said, "I talked to George last night. He thought it would be a good idea."

Doris placed the picture on the desk, turned, and walked to the door, looking back at Forman as she exited, closing the door behind her. As Doris approached her office, she saw Joe Everton and Robert Cleary standing in the hallway talking. When they saw her, they both approached her and Joe taking her arm said, "My God, Doris, are you alright? We heard what happened last night. It certainly was a good thing that Forman happened along. George already has security in the parking lot. They will be there twenty four hours a day and every day. What a terrible thing to happen."

"I guess Albert did save me from some serious damage. Thank you for coming down to check on me." She looked at Robert, who was shuffling from one foot to the other not saying anything, and she finally said, "Thank you, Robert, for coming down to check on me."

"Yeah, right. I got to go," Robert said, "I'm just glad nothing happened to you. After all, who would run the advertising campaign?" And with that he turned and walked away.

Joe said, "When I told him what happened, he said he was going to send his sister and Bea to check on you. I think you have impressed him. I am really glad you are alright, Doris." And Joe then turned and left.

When Doris entered her office the girls rushed to her, patting her shoulder, holding her hand, and demanding a blow-by-blow description of what happened. There were a lot of oohs and aahs as she told her story. When she finished she said, "Alright, enough of this drama. Let's get back to work." But there was not too much work getting done that morning. Every few minutes someone else came in demanding a recount of what happened, and Doris patiently described the event to each one as they came into her office.

CHAPTER 19

At six o'clock Carmen arrived at Lazarus' apartment and rang the bell. Lazarus opened the door, stepped back and Carmen entered. "Now listen to me," Lazarus barked, "there is no cooking, nothing. Woo is coming over here in a little while for a meeting. I don't want him to know you are here. Don't make any noise. Do not come out unless I call you. Do you understand?"

Carmen, nodded her head, turned, and walked into the kitchen. She went over to the chair at the table, sat down, put her arms on the table and lay her head on her arms, and closed her eyes.

Thirty minutes later Stanley Woo was at Lazarus' apartment door. He knocked and waited for Lazarus to open the door. When nothing happened he knocked again, a little harder this time, and waited. When no one answered the door, he shrugged his shoulders, turned, went back to the elevator, and pushed the button. Just as the elevator arrived Lazarus opened the apartment door and said, "Woo, where the hell are you going?"

Woo answered, "I knocked twice and no one answered. I thought you forget and weren't home."

"Woo, damn it," Lazarus scowled, "I don't forget. I was in the bathroom. Now get in here and sit down. We have a lot of talking to do."

"Is Bernard screwing up? I thought we had him in our pocket when he left here."

"Sit down, shut up, and listen," Lazarus said, and Woo sat down on the sofa. Lazarus stood over him and said, "Pick up the telephone and dial this number." He read from a sheet of paper in his hand. Woo picked up the phone and dialed. When the phone answered, he heard a beeping noise and a voice said, "The number dialed is not a working number. Please check your listing and dial again." Woo put down the phone and said, "It's not a working number."

99

"Oh," said Lazarus in surprise, "Try this number." He then read a second number from the page. Woo again dialed and got the same message as before.

Woo looked a little confused when he asked, "What kind of numbers are you giving me? What kind of game are you playing?"

Lazarus ignored him, and this time gave a number from memory. Woo did not move. "Dial the God damned number." Lazarus barked and repeated the number. Woo dialed and the phone was answered, "You have reached Metal Fabricators. The offices are now closed. Please leave your name and address and your call will be returned. Thank you." Woo then heard a dial tone. He hung up the phone and looked at Lazarus. Lazarus shook his head back and forth and said, "Now dial this number," and he repeated a second number by memory. Woo did not move. Lazarus stuck his face very close to Woo's face and repeated the number, then stood back up. Woo slowly picked up the phone and dialed, and when the phone was answered, he heard this message, "You have reached Master Iron Works. The offices are now closed. Please leave your name and address and your call will be returned. Thank you."

Lazarus took a step back not moving his eyes from Woo. "Woo," He said, "you are such a fucking imbecile. Do you have any idea what just happened? What is your head full of? Chinese shit noodles?" Lazarus then took a step forward and swung his arm in a full ark, slapping Woo on the side of his head with such force, that he flipped over the arm of the couch and onto the floor. As Woo started to move Lazarus kicked Woo in the ribs, shouting, "You're so damn dumb, you don't deserve to be alive. Now, you idiot, do you have any idea what is going on?"

Woo lay on the floor looking up at Lazarus not moving, opened his mouth and said, "I thought you weren't giving me my share."

"Your share!" Lazarus exploded, "You dumb piece of chicken shit. Your share is what I say it is. Your unbelievable stupidity could have cost us the whole deal by using Chinese year names for the companies and printing non-working phone numbers on the invoices. I didn't check the addresses, but they probably don't exist. Am I right?"

At this point Woo rolled over and got to his hands and knees trying to get up. Lazarus came over and slammed his foot onto Woo's

100

hand breaking several bones. Woo groaned, fell back down and passed out. Several minutes elapsed and Woo started groaning again. Lazarus shouted, "Get up, you piece of shit. Get up." This time, Lazarus just prodded him with his foot. Slowly, Woo opened his eyes and in a faint whisper said, "Please let me up. I can explain the whole thing."

Lazarus stepped back and said, "Get up, you ignorant asshole."

Woo, slowly got to his knees, holding his broken hand to his chest, and with his good hand pulled himself up to sit on the couch.

Lazarus said, "Did you ever hear of Dragon Iron Purveyors? Did you ever hear of Tiger Steel Company? Are you some kind of an idiot to think I wouldn't find out you were stealing from the company. I set up a foolproof scheme that is going to make us rich and you do your dumb ass act to blow the whole thing. Well, dumb ass, what do you have to say?"

Woo slumped over, his head leaning on the coffee table, his good hand slowly raising his pant leg. Woo pulled a small pistol from an ankle holster, sat up, and pointed it at Lazarus.

Lazarus took a small step backwards and held his hands out to his sides saying, "Woo, are you about to do something really stupid? If you shoot me, you are going to jail for embezzlement and to the electric chair for murder."

"Listen, Brenton," Woo started, his voice barely above a whisper but steady, "I thought you were screwing me by only giving me a quarter of what we take. Now, since you think I am such a fucking idiot, I really do think you are screwing me. I may not be as smart as you are, you asshole, but I am smart enough to kill you and to continue to bleed the company."

"Woo, I am not screwing you. I told you that there were other people involved in our little scheme to compensate ourselves for what we should be making. A move like yours could alert the company and could cause an audit that would end our little game." Lazarus slowly lowered his hands to his sides and slowly moved one foot forward. "You keep the money from Dragon Iron and Tiger Steel but those companies must disappear. Just remember that everything points to you. If we take too much, we can be caught and you will go to jail for embezzling. If you kill me, everything will be over."

101

Lazarus leaped across the coffee table at Woo trying to grab the gun. Woo pulled the trigger, the bullet hit Lazarus square in the chest and he landed draped over the coffee table, dead.

When the shouting started, Carmen raised her head and sat listening. She did not move until she heard the gunshots. She quietly got up, went into the laundry alcove, and sat down on the far side of the washing machine. When she heard the kitchen door open, she opened her mouth wide, silently sucking in air. When she heard the door close, she slowly and silently let the air out of her lungs and otherwise didn't move.

Woo closed the kitchen door satisfied that no one was there. He then went to the bedroom, walked around the room and not finding anyone in the apartment, calmly walked back to the living room. He sat in the chair next to Lazarus' body, bent over, and laid the gun on the floor. He raised his pant leg over the ankle holster and slid in the gun. Woo then walked to the apartment door and looked out the peephole. Seeing the hallway empty he slowly opened the door, walked out, closed the door, went to the elevator, and pushed the button. When the door opened, he entered the empty elevator car and was gone.

Carmen sat behind the washing machine, not moving, for an hour, then slowly got up and moved to the kitchen door. She pushed it open enough to look through to the living room. From the kitchen door she could not see anyone, so, she slowly opened the door and walked into the room. When she saw Lazarus lying, sprawled over the coffee table, blood oozing from his side, she lost her breath, fell to the floor and sat there for several minutes. Slowly, she got up and went to Lazarus. She bent over, and gently shook his shoulder. When he didn't move she straightened up, crossed herself, and went back into the kitchen. Picking up her sweater and purse from behind the washing machine, she took out a ring of keys. She took a single key, went to the apartment door, looked through the peephole and seeing no one in the hallway opened the door, went out and closed it. With that single key, she turned the dead bolt lock. She hurried to the elevator and pushed the call button. When the elevator door opened, she entered the empty elevator car and rode to the ground floor. She walked out of the building without seeing anyone. As she approached her car, she threw the single key into the wooded area next to the paved lot.

Carmen started her car, crossed herself, and said, "Thank you, Jesus." And slowly drove home.

As soon as Carmen got home, she kissed her little boy on the top of his head, went to the phone, and called Deana Zimmer, her immediate boss. When Deana answered, Carmen, trying to control her crying, spoke into the phone, "Deana, something terrible has happened. Please come to your office right away. It's terrible. Please come right away."

Deana answered, "Carmen, what is it? Are you alright? Tell me what happened?"

"No, no. I can't, please come to your office right away. I have something to tell you and it is horrible. I will be in your office in twenty five minutes. Please come, it's horrible." At this, Carmen put down the phone, turned to her mother and said, "I have to go back to work." She then picked up her pocketbook and, without another word, rushed out of her house.

When Deana arrived at the Stylex offices she found Carmen in a chair by her desk crying. "Carmen," she said, "what is wrong? What happened? Are you hurt?"

"Oh, Deana, I don't know what to do. Lazarus has been making me come to his apartment, get undressed, and serve him supper and then he makes me have sex with him."

"Oh my God!" Deana yelled, "That is insane. Why would you let him do this to you?"

Carmen held up her hand, took a breath, and then said, "My mother and brother are both illegal aliens. Mr. Lazarus found out and threatened to turn them into the immigration office unless I did everything he asked of me."

Deana stood, shaking her head, her mouth open, when she finally spoke. "Carmen, why are you telling me all this now? What happened?"

Carmen, almost finished crying, said, "Mr. Lazarus is dead. Mr. Woo shot him and killed him. It happened about two hours ago. They were arguing about stealing money from the company. They were making me help them steal from the company. Now my family will have to go back to Brazil. We are all going to die. I don't know what to do." And she started crying all over again.

Deana grabbed Carmen by the arm, pulled her up, and said, "You are not going to be fired. I am taking you to George's house. You will tell him everything. He will know what to do. Now stop crying and come with me."

Deana half walked Carmen and half dragged her until they got to Deana's car where Carmen was dumped into the front seat. Deana then got into the car and headed out of the parking lot. She headed for George Stillwell's house. When they arrived and George opened the door, Deana blurted out, "Lazarus is dead. Carmen has to tell you the whole story. Pulling Carmen through the door, she dragged her into the house and dropped her in a chair in the family's den room.

George came in behind them saying "What do you mean Lazarus is dead? Did Carmen kill Lazarus? What the hell is going on?"

Deana turned, and said, "George, Carmen is going to tell you a story that is hard to believe. After you hear it, you have to decide if we should call the police, or what."

George turned to look at Carmen, who was now crying with abandon. "Carmen," He said, "I will make everything all right. Now calm yourself and tell me everything that happened." Carmen looked up and saw George looking down at her, smiling gently.

She then took a big sigh and started speaking. She told George that about a year ago Mr. Lazarus found out about her family's immigration problem and how he made her steal from the company. She told how he was doing a whole bunch of terrible things to her.

After hearing the whole story, George stood up shaking his head and turning back to Deana said, "You are certainly right. That is an unbelievable story." Turning back to Carmen, he said, "You are not going to be fired. I will send an attorney to your home tomorrow night at seven o'clock. You will give her all the papers you have about your immigration problems, and she will fix it so your whole family will be legal in the United States. Carmen, I would appreciate you not saying a word to anyone about this. Deana I will take care of calling the authorities about the shooting tomorrow morning."

***

Earlier that day, the play date with Anna's nieces and Doris' two girls was going on, and the girls were having a blast. When Doris arrived holding two apple pies, she was let in by Anna and led into the dining room where she was just starting to set the table. There were two china plates on opposite sides of the table with the plastic plates on either side of the china plates for the girls. There were also china plates at each end of the table where Anna was just placing silverware.

"Oh, are you expecting company tonight?" DD asked.

"Well, not exactly company. You will at last get to meet my brother, who finally, is not tied up with work. My aunt is also coming over."

"Well," Doris said, "I guess I will finally meet the traveling salesman. I didn't even know you had an aunt living here. But I guess I already know your family secrets. You are having Robert and Bea?"

"Yes, that's it." laughed Anna, "My Aunt Bea has a boyfriend that keeps her pretty busy, and my brother Bobby, who I guess you already know is Robert, always has to travel around to make sure his salesmen are doing what salesmen should be doing. But tonight, you will officially meet both of them."

While the girls played in the living room, Doris and Anna went into the kitchen and finished getting the food ready for the table. Doris came out rounding up the girls for the before dinner bathroom break. After washing and drying the girls' hands, she led them out to the dining room. She was laughing as she walked into the room, only to stop in mid stride. When she saw Robert Cleary and Bea Patterson sitting at each end of the table she said, "Well, it is about time I met Bobby and Aunt Bea in person."

Robert looked up and when he saw Doris, he quickly got out of his chair. "What are you doing here?" he asked,

Anna, smiling, said, "Robert, Doris already knows Bobby and Robert and Aunt Bea. But I think this is the first time you are meeting DD."

Robert, after a minute, sat back down, all four girls had taken their seats and were looking at the adults waiting to start the meal.

"Well", Robert said, "I think meeting you, DD, is going to be one of the happiest days of my life."

Bea said, "The children are ready to eat." And turning to the children she said, "I am Aunt Bea. What are your names?"

CHAPTER 20

At ten A.M., Robert followed by Forman, walked in to George Stillwell's office. Grace looked up, smiled and said, "Good morning, gentlemen, go right in, he is waiting for you."

When they entered, George greeted them and told them to sit down in the three chairs in front of his desk, leaving the middle chair vacant. When Robert started to speak, George held up his hand and Robert stopped. A few minutes later, Woo was ushered in by Grace, who then closed the door.

Woo looking around said, "George, what do you want from me?"

George said, "Woo, just sit down in that empty chair and listen to me. Lazarus was shot and killed by an unknown assailant yesterday. However, we have a pretty good idea who that assailant is." Woo stood up, but before he could say anything, George screamed at him, "SIT DOWN." With that, Woo sank back to his chair.

"Carmen is no longer going to prepare checks to the phony suppliers Lazarus and you have created. Carmen's mother and brother are now getting green cards. I have prepared a letter for you to sign. It says you are leaving the company today for personnel reasons and are relinquishing all benefits that might accrue to you. Do you have any questions?"

Woo sat still for a minute, then leaned forward, took the pen from the desk, and signed the letter. Robert took the letter and signed it. He handed it across to Forman, who also signed it and gave it back to George.

George took the letter and said, "Woo, I strongly suggest you be out of this building within the hour. I strongly suggest you go back to your home country before you get charged with murder. Forman will escort you out of the building."

Woo stood up, turned, and walked out of the office followed by Forman. It was quiet for a moment, and then George said, "OK, I guess that is the end of an ugly story. Let's get back to work"

"Yeah," Robert said, "I really look forward to spending a lot of time with one of your new employees. I really never knew DD Wilcox until last night. I have a lot of catching up to do." Before George could respond, Robert was gone, on the way to Doris's office.

When he entered Doris' office he put his fingers to his lips to stop either of the girls from greeting him, walked to the door marked Manager, and knocked. There was an immediate answer, "Come in." He opened the door and said, "Is DD here?" There was a big laugh from Doris, sitting at her desk. "Yes," she said, "I think DD will be around if Bobby needs her, and even for Robert if he has the nerve to show up."

"Well," Robert said, "Bobby would just like to take DD to dinner tonight and apologize for his atrocious behavior recently. Oh, and he would like to invite Doris to come along." Doris still smiling said, "DD and Doris will be happy to have supper with Bobby, as long as he brings Robert along." Robert laughed, "Robert will be there to pick up the check, and I think the four of us will have a super time. I mean a real super time."

Three months later Doris married Robert. The four little girls were finally sisters, and the family settled in to the perfect home in the perfect neighborhood with the white picket fence.

List of characters

George Stillwell	President and founder
Joseph Everton	Chief Executive Officer
Brenton Lazarus	Asst. Chief Executive Officer
Stanley Horworth	Chief Financial Officer
Stanley Woo	Asst. Chief Financial Officer
Dietmar Wertzer	Production Manager
William (Bill) Bernard	Union Rep. - Factory Worker
Robert (Bobby) Cleary	Sales Manager (daughters Mary and Joan)
Doris (DD) Wilcox	Marketing and Public Relations (daughters Mary, Susan)
Beatrice Patterson	Secretary to Robert Cleary (Aunt)
Deana Zimmer	Accounting Dept. Manager
Susan Butler	Accounting Dept. - Accts Rec.
Carmen Mendez	Accounting Dept. - Accts Pay/Payroll
Frances Pestic	Accounting Dept. - General Ledger
Robin Taylor	Marketing Manager
Brenda Vogel	Advertising Manager
Grace Sutton	Everton's secretary (and daughter)
Anna Maxwell	Robert Cleary's sister (nanny to his kids)
Alice Donald	Pauline's secretary
Betty English	Factory Floor Inspector (Bill Bernard's girlfriend

Morton Erstling

May 29-1931

May 30-2013

About The Author

Often called "Mort," he started his career as a Certified Public Accountant and an Attorney. When the cruise industry was in its early childhood, he was Comptroller and Chief Operating Officer of Eastern Steamship Lines, which ran cruises to the Caribbean from Miami, Florida. After 18 years, he decided to form his own concession company providing professional services to the industry and operating this company together with his wife for 10 years. Upon relocating to Tallahassee, Fl., he dusted off his law degree, and started Big Bend Title Company that operated until his retirement.

Thereupon, he let his intellectual and artistic sides take over. He proceeded to earn three more bachelor degrees one in studio arts, & one in chemical engineering. He wrote two books of poetry and this current novella. He was a man of many talents and appeared with little theater groups both in Miami and Tallahassee. A true renaissance man was he.

Maria Beltran of Readers Favorite stated, "Thrilling from start to finish, "Danger in Blackwater Swamp" is a novel that lovers of suspense, drama and a bit of romance may not want to miss out on."

BJ Hathaway, a single woman living on the St. Marks River in North Florida, discovers someone digging in her backyard during the night...the perpetrator -- Jake Collins, a longtime foe, kidnaps her, then leaves her for dead, trapped in a sinkhole. BJ must defeat her nemesis or lose her own life.

Will she survive?

www.ingramcontent.com/pod-product-compliance
Lightning Source LLC
Chambersburg PA
CBHW030635130626
46552CB00002B/866